in the palm
of darkness

in the palm
of darkness

A NOVEL

Mayra Montero

translated from the Spanish by Edith Grossman

HarperFlamingo
An Imprint of HarperCollinsPublishers

Originally published in Spain as *Tú, la Oscuridad* by Tusquets Editores, S.A., Barcelona.

A hardcover edition of this book was published in 1997 by HarperCollins Publishers.

HarperCollins books may be purchased for educational, business, or sales promotional use. For information, please e-mail the Special Markets Department at SPsales@harpercollins.com.

First HarperFlamingo edition published 1998.

Designed by Ruth Lee

The Library of Congress has catalogued the hardcover edition as follows:

Montero, Mayra.
    [Tú, la oscuridad. English]
    In the palm of darkness : a novel / Mayra Montero : translated from the Spanish by Edith Grossman. — 1st ed.
       p. cm.
    ISBN 0-06-018703-4
    I. Grossman, Edith. II. Title.
PQ7440.M56T813   1997
863—dc20   96-41303

ISBN 0-06-092906-5 (pbk.)

HB 02.26.2018

❈❈❈ CONTENTS ❈❈❈

✕❋✕ O N E ✕❋✕
Blue Sheep

A Tibetan astrologer told Martha I would die by fire.

I thought of it as soon as Thierry began talking about the feasts of his childhood. It was a gratuitous association, since he was really trying to tell me the name of a fruit he had tasted only once in his life, when he was still a little boy and had suffered an attack of what I think was malaria, and to comfort him his father brought this rare treat to his bed. From the description, I assumed it was a pear. Thierry chuckled quietly: That fruit reminded him of a young girl's flesh, and he had never again held anything like it between his lips.

We were lying in the underbrush and I let him talk a while. It's impossible to keep a man like Thierry quiet for long. We had just recorded the voice of a superb specimen, a tiny frog with a blue abdomen that lets itself be seen only one week during the year, and I was thinking that the joy of having captured the sound helped me to be tolerant. Perhaps it was joy and not the story about the pear that forced me to think of death, *my death*, and what

Martha had been told in Dharmsala. "He said my husband would be burned to death"—I could hear her voice, furious because I had suggested there must have been some misunderstanding—"and as far as I know, you're the only husband I have."

Thierry was still waxing nostalgic about how well you could eat in Jérémie thirty or forty years ago, and I concluded it was pretty ironic for anyone to prophesy that kind of death for me considering how much time I spent submerged in ponds and lagoons, drenched by downpours in swamps, crawling along riverbanks, my mouth full of mud and my eyelids rimmed with mosquitoes. I said as much to Martha.

"That's no guarantee," she replied, happy to contradict me. "A person can burn to death in an airplane, a hotel room, even on a boat, you know, when you're right on the water ..."

Martha brought a coat home from Dharmsala. It was a gift from Barbara, the friend who made the trip with her. It was too coarse for my taste, but she claimed it was made from the wool of the blue sheep, and had I ever heard of that sheep? It was the favorite meal of the snow leopard. I stared at her and she returned my gaze: The coat was the best proof that Martha herself had become Barbara's favorite meal.

When you're in a profession like mine, it's very easy to catch certain signals, identify certain odors, recognize the movements that announce imminent amplexus (the term used for sexual congress between frogs). Martha refused to have me go with her on that trip—years before, when we were first married, we often talked about traveling to India some day—but she didn't say it like that, she calculated first and said it with even greater cruelty, if that's possible: Since I had to fly to Nashville for my conference—she said "your conference"—she'd take off a couple of weeks and travel with her best friend. She avoided mentioning the place they'd be visiting, and I went along with it, swearing to myself I wouldn't ask a single question, and gradually my suspicions were confirmed: by the brochures that suddenly appeared in the house, by a couple of books on the Hindustanic Plate—Barbara is a geologist—and finally by the plane tickets. Martha kept them in her briefcase, then one night decided to take them out and leave them on the big table in the study; she obviously intended me to find them there, look at them without saying a word, and understand. One needs a lot of understanding.

Shortly before Martha left, she told me she had put a list of the hotels where she'd be staying, and the approximate dates, on the computer. She laughed and said she had used the file name "Hindu Voyage," and I pretended I hadn't heard. At the last minute she wouldn't let me go to the airport with her; a friend of Barbara's had offered to take them both, and so we said good-bye at home—that same night I was flying to Nashville—with no insinuations or reproaches. I assumed that any attempt to ask for an explanation would only be humiliating for me.

Thierry often says that the bad thing isn't if a man feels afraid to die, the really bad thing is if a man never thinks about death at all. He doesn't say it in those words, he uses other words, probably better ones. Thierry's eloquence is solemn, profound, almost biblical. When Martha returned, much later than planned, she brought back the blue sheep coat as if it were a trophy, along with a smoldering certainty about the kind of death awaiting me in my present life—she emphasized the phrase "your present life." Then I realized that during the whole time we had been separated, the possibility that she was somehow leaving me had never entered my mind. Just to be polite, she asked about the response to my paper, but I didn't have a chance to answer, there was an interruption, a telephone call for her. She talked briefly and came back, even felt obliged to try a second time: How did it go in Nashville?

The idea for this expedition had, in fact, surfaced in Nashville, but I didn't tell her so. A few hours before I was due to leave for home, I had received a dinner invitation, a white card with an engraved drawing of a small gray frog: Professor Vaughan Patterson, the eminent Australian herpetologist, would expect me at eight at the Mère Bulles restaurant, and would I please be punctual.

I was so flattered that I did something extraordinary: I rummaged through my suitcase to see if I had a clean shirt and jacket. At seven sharp I walked out of the hotel and started down Commerce Street, which leads directly to Second Avenue, right across from the restaurant. It was a short distance, it wouldn't take me more than fifteen or twenty minutes, but I wanted to be there before Patterson arrived. He was known as an impatient man with a short temper and sheer contempt for colleagues who talked to him about anything but amphibians. Yet all of them would have fought for the privilege of sitting at his table. Patterson was the greatest living authority on everything having to do with the African anurans; his work with the Tasmanian axolotl was legendary, and he boasted of keeping alive, when the species was already considered extinct, the last specimen of *Taudactylus diurnus*, sole survivor of the colony that he himself had bred in his laboratory in Adelaide.

When I walked into the restaurant, forty minutes early, Patterson was already there. He smiled timidly, you might almost say sadly, congratulated me on my paper, and offered me a seat beside him. I noticed that he had skin like cellophane, and frail, small, rather stiff hands. With one of them he began to draw on his napkin. I watched him become engrossed in sketching a frog, he didn't even look up when the waiter brought his drink. *Eleutherodactylus sanguineus* he wrote in small letters when he was finished, framing the name between the animal's paws. He handed me the drawing.

"Help me look for it," he whispered. "If there are any left, they're on the Mont des Infants Perdus in Haiti."

Then he fell silent and began to look at the river. From the windows of the Mère Bulles you can see the waters of the Cumberland River and, from time to time, a nostalgic steamboat. One of them, called the *Belle Carol*, sailed past just then. I was so astonished by his request that I deliberately concentrated on the drawing. Patterson became aware of this and took back the napkin.

"I don't have the time or the health to search for it," he murmured. "Did you hear that I have leukemia?"

I shook my head. We had been introduced three years earlier at the conference in Canterbury; at the time we barely exchanged a dozen sentences, and later we were both on the same panel discussing the disappearance of the *Litoria aurea*. We had talked only of frogs, nothing but frogs.

Patterson folded the napkin and patted his lips, ruining the sketch, of course. Then he made his offer: If I agreed to undertake the expedition in the fall, the biology department at his university would cover all the costs. And as soon as I brought him a specimen of *Eleutherodactylus sanguineus* ("I'll settle for one"), they would grant me a two-year fellowship for research on the subject of my choice, anywhere I wanted to go. It went without saying, he emphasized, that he expected an immediate reply.

At this point I ought to mention that Martha is a very suspicious woman; her profession also allows her to detect the smallest, most fleeting sign of instability or danger. She slowly realized that something significant had happened in Nashville, perhaps something having to do with my paper, and the danger lay in my not telling her about it.

From then on her interest stopped being merely polite and took on all the ferocity of a siege: She questioned me about every detail of the conference, about the other speakers and the subjects under discussion; she tried to find out if something important had been said, an unexpected announcement, one of those bombs that are suddenly dropped in the middle of a paper and leave everyone speechless. Did I remember the time Corben seemed so circumspect and then came out with his findings on the incubation of *Rheobatrachus silus?*

Of course I remembered. Martha was capable of resorting to any kind of trick to get the secret out of me. She knew the allusion to Corben touched certain coiled springs of memory, memory and rivalry, things that are sometimes confused in the heart of a frog hunter, a researcher who wants to get there first, get in the first shot, before anybody else. She was trying to find out what had happened in Nashville, and to do that she would play dirty, root through my jealousies, search out my petty disappointments and failures. Corben was a genius who had been lucky.

On the other hand, her interest obviously did not come as a complete surprise to me: Martha was also what you might call a woman of science. We had already chosen different fields before we were married; she had decided on marine biology. "Instead of a division of property," she would say to her friends, "Victor and I are making a division of fauna." But she always kept up with my work, and was a meticulous collaborator from the time I began to accumulate data regarding the disappearances.

At first we avoided calling it by that name and used less violent words: "Decline" was my favorite, amphibian populations were "declining"; entire colonies of healthy toads went into permanent hiding; the same frogs we had grown tired of hearing only a season earlier fell silent and became rare; they sickened and died, or simply fled, and no one could explain where or why.

But her questions about what had happened in Nashville revealed a different kind of interest, a perverse delight in trivial details that went beyond simple scientific curiosity. Of course I didn't mention my meeting with Patterson; she was the one who asked if I had seen the Australian. I was careful to ask which Australian she meant, which of the dozens of herpetologists who had come from Melbourne, Sidney, Canberra. Yet it made no sense to carry it too far. I had to be aware that the Australian, the only possible Australian she was interested in, was the venerated Vaughan Patterson.

Two months later she accidentally learned about the upcoming expedition. The professor who was going to replace me at the laboratory called to give me some information about another Haitian species that hadn't been seen for many years. Martha wrote down the name of the frog, *Eleutherodactylus lamprotes*, carefully noted all the data, and typed them on a small card. Across the bottom she wrote in longhand: "Don't you think Haiti is a dangerous place for field trips?"

I copied the information for my files and gave her back the card with another sentence written below hers: "Your astrologer already said I would die over a slow fire somewhere in the world."

Between 1974 and 1982, the *Bufo boreas boreas*, better known as the Western toad, disappeared from the Colorado mountains and from almost all its other American habitats.

According to studies carried out by Dr. Cynthia Carey, professor of biology at the University of Colorado, the cause of its disappearance was a massive infection attributed to the bacteria *Aeromonas hidrophila*. The infection produces acute hemorrhaging, especially in the legs, which take on a reddish coloring, giving rise to the name of the illness: Red Leg Disease.

A healthy toad should not succumb to an *Aeromonas* infection. But in the case of *Bufo boreas boreas*, there was a failure of the immune system.

The cause of the failure is unknown.

✠✠ T W O ✠✠

Bombardopolis

My father never called me by name. What you love you respect, he said, and there is no need to name what you love.

He learned this from his father, who did not call him by name either. It was an ancient custom, something that came with the first man, with the first father of a father of my father who came to this land from Guinea.

My father was named Thierry, like me, and he had a very difficult job, the most difficult one ever known: He was a hunter, he was what they call a *pwazon rat*, that is what those hunters were called.

My mother, whose name was Claudine, had her hands full taking care of us, her five children. We lived in Jérémie, not right in the city but in a shantytown near the port. We learned to swim there, that was where we learned to fish. Haiti was a different place in those days. The sea too was wider, or deeper, or more loved by the fish, and from that sea we took our food, white-fleshed fish with short spines that brought joy to the entire fam-

10

ily. We also had a pen for pigs, the kind they call brown devil pigs, and when a litter was born we feasted in our house. One suckling was set aside and sacrificed to the Baron. My mother was a devotee of Baron-la-Croix, and my father had to be one too because of his profession.

You want to know where the frogs go. I cannot say, sir, but let me ask you a question: Where did our fish go? Almost all of them left this sea, and in the forest the wild pigs disappeared, and the migratory ducks, and even the iguanas for eating, they went too. Just take a look at what's left of humans, take a careful look: You can see the bones pushing out under their skins as if they wanted to escape, to leave behind that weak flesh where they are so battered, to go into hiding someplace else.

At times I think, but keep it to myself, I think that one day a man like you will come here, someone who crosses the ocean to look for a couple of frogs, and when I say frogs, I mean any creature, and he will find only a great hill of bones on the shore, a hill higher than the peak of Tête Boeuf. Then he will say to himself, Haiti is finished, God Almighty, those bones are all that remain.

On Sundays Papa would bring us sweets. He bought them at a drugstore that used to be in Jérémie, a place filled with odds and ends and smells, it was called Pharmacie du Bord de Mer and sold more candy than medicine, nobody took medicine in those days. The owner was a skinny man with sunken eyes, and ears that faced forward like a sick dog's, and a tiny, fleshy mouth, a mouth like a chicken's ass that never opened even to say good morning. He inherited the drugstore from his mother, who was scalded to death in syrup. This happened before I was born, but I know that everybody in

Jérémie mourned her, brought candles and drums to the funeral, called down the *loas*, the fire spirits, and the mourning lasted many days.

This is how the accident happened: A woman who worked for Madame Christine, for that was the owner's name, was walking back and forth carrying sacks of bottles, and she happened to trip on one of them, tried to steady herself on the edge of the stove, but instead she grabbed onto the big pot where that day's syrups were cooking. Madame Christine was squatting next to the stove, pouring some milk for her cat. They were both bathed in disaster: She did not move, she was cooked on the spot, she didn't even drop the pitcher of milk that must have boiled in the heat; the cat ran off to die in the underbrush.

The first time they told me that story I was very little, but the first thing I asked was what had happened to the woman carrying the sack of bottles. That's a defect of mine when people tell me something: I always keep track of the ones in the background, the ones who disappear for no reason, the forgotten ones. Everybody talked about Madame Christine and her kitty, but let's see, whatever happened to the woman who worked for her? Did she fall down too and burn her back? Did she get up and run after the cat, or did she slowly creep over to her dead employer, take the pitcher from her hands, and blow on the milk to separate the cream?

My older brother was named Jean Pierre, and he was born a little lame. In fact, we were born together, we were twins, but the midwife took Jean Pierre out first and was in such a hurry she hurt one of his ankles. A year later Yoyotte came into the world, the only girl my mother had, and they gave her that name in honor of her godmother, who was a cook from Bombardopolis, a town up north where my father used to spend a lot of time. A little while later my brother Etienne was born, and it wasn't until many more years had gone by that Paul, our youngest brother, finally made his appearance.

When my sister's godmother came to see us, we had the feasts I told you about. My father invited his brothers; my mother invited her female cousins, because her brothers and sisters were all dead; and the cousins brought their own children, who were our age, and the house filled with music and dancing and shouting, and Yoyotte Placide, the most famous cook in Bombardopolis, began to sing and beat egg whites for meringues. I still remember her song:

Solèy, o, Moin pa moun isit o, solèy,
Moin sé nég ginin, solèy,
M'pa kab travesé, solèy,
Min batiman-m chaviré, solèy.

It was a very sad song: "Oh, Sun, I'm not from here, Sun, I was born in Guinea and can never go back, oh, Sun, my boat sank," but she sang it as if it were the most joyful thing. Yoyotte Placide always said there was no way to make a good meringue if you didn't sing to the yolks that had been left behind, the ones you were saving for the omelette. You had to keep the rooster's seed happy. Then she showed us a red dot in the middle of the yolk: That's where the song went in, that's where the order came back for the whites, mixed together in a separate bowl, to let themselves be whipped into foam; that's how you made meringue.

My father's brothers drank the rum called Barbancourt,

and from time to time my mother's cousins raised the bottle too. One of them, named Frou-Frou, lifted her skirt and began to dance. My mother scolded her, but she paid no attention; we children sat on the floor facing her and applauded when Frou-Frou twirled around. My father applauded too, sometimes he would dance with her, he grabbed her by the waist and they spun around together, but then my mother would come out of the kitchen and separate them, and we children would applaud some more because by then Frou-Frou's blouse had opened and suddenly out popped her two breasts, so big and light-skinned. The other cousins came running to stop my mother from hitting her, and Frou-Frou fell down, she lay on the floor on her back and began to moan, then we saw something jump around in her stomach and go down toward her groin and we children thought she had eaten a toad—excuse me, I know you don't like jokes about those creatures—and the women held her down and shook her a little to keep her from taking off all her clothes.

My father would get angry because he hated for my mother to scold him in front of his brothers; he left the house in a rage and walked around for a while looking at the ocean and swallowing mouthfuls of rum. After a while Frou-Frou began to calm down, she had a little girl named Carmelite who put cold cloths on her forehead and helped her comb her hair. My mother swore she would never invite her to our house again, but the months would go by, and when my sister's godmother sent word that she was coming, everything was forgotten and Frou-Frou arrived for the feast.

As time passed, she stopped putting on a show. We children would ask her to dance and she would shake her head and smile. Instead she would go to peel vegetables by the pigpens, she would toss the parings to the brown devil pigs and grow dreamy as she watched them eat.

Yoyotte, my sister, wanted to be a cook just like her godmother and set up a business in Jérémie like the one the other Yoyotte had in Bombardopolis. Yoyotte Placide was not opposed to her goddaughter learning the trade, but instead of opening a business in Jérémie, she encouraged her to come to Bombardopolis and help at her own food stand. "Sooner or later it will be yours," she would say, because Yoyotte Placide had no children and was too old by then to ever have any.

All of this was talked about at the table while we ate our fish soup, and my mother fumed because she didn't want them to take her only daughter away to Bombardopolis. Nobody wants to lose her little girl, she would say, who would take care of her and her husband later on? My brother Etienne, who was a very sweet-natured boy, put down his spoon and promised that he would take care of them both. Jean Pierre, my older brother, burst out laughing and called him a faggot. My mother finally gave vent to her feelings and smacked each of us, even me, though I hadn't said anything, while she glared at Yoyotte's godmother with hatred. Sometimes the discussion grew heated and my father would stand up, kick away his chair, and bite his lips, a sign that at any moment he would put an end to the feast. Since nobody wanted that to happen, we were all quiet except Frou-Frou, who walked in and out of the kitchen chirping like a little bird, asking my father if he'd like more squash, or asking my mother if it was time to serve the dessert, which was almost always papaya in syrup or pan sugar with guava.

One afternoon during Holy Week, while we were still sitting at the table, Frou-Frou went out to the pen to feed scraps to the pigs, and her little girl, Carmelite, announced that soon she would have a brother, just like we did. The other women made a great fuss, and my mother barely managed to bring her hands up to her chest. My father's brothers stood to ask him if it was true, then they began to laugh and embrace him, patting him on the back to congratulate him. My father laughed too, but in a very strange way, with his eyes fixed on Yoyotte Placide, his cook from Bombardopolis, who had lowered her head and looked grief-stricken.

Frou-Frou didn't come back to our house for a long time. My mother invited her, but Yoyotte Placide threatened to scratch out her eyes if she ever saw her again. And no one dared to doubt Yoyotte Placide's threats, much less defy her orders: She was the one who brought the food, she was the one who cooked it, without Yoyotte Placide there was no party, and my father and mother both knew it. But Carmelite, Frou-Frou's daughter, still came by. My mother, who was a fair woman when she wasn't angry, told us all that the little girl was not to blame for what her lunatic mother did, and she invited her, like always, and treated her the same, or almost the same, except that she never allowed her to speak of the baby who was on the way.

The last feast I remember was a farewell banquet for my sister. She had just turned eleven, and following the wishes of her godmother, she was going to live in Bombardopolis to learn the trade and work at the food stand that would one day be hers. My mother cried all night, but then she became very happy at the table, especially when she saw Carmelite carrying in her little brother so we could all meet him. My father told Jean Pierre and me, because we were the oldest, that the infant was also our brother and would be living with us from now on.

When Yoyotte Placide finally left for Bombardopolis with her goddaughter, my father ran over to Carmelite, snatched the baby out of her arms, and put him down on my sister's bed, which was now free. Carmelite didn't seem very sad, just the opposite, she told Jean Pierre and me that the child cried too much and it was a relief to give him away.

Later we found out it had all been arranged before the feast. My mother began to care for the infant as if he was her own, though Frou-Frou came by from time to time and helped her wash diapers and prepare his pap.

They named the boy Julien, but my father never called him by name.

✖◇✖ THREE ✖◇✖
The Light of the World

I began taping my conversations with Thierry when I realized that between stories he was inserting important information about the frog. The last time he had seen the *Eleutherodactylus sanguineus* was not on the Mont des Enfants Perdus but at the top of Casetaches Hill, a steep, rocky elevation near Jérémie, his hometown.

He said this right from the start. The same Haitian professor who had recommended him brought him to my hotel in Port-au-Prince, introduced us without much ceremony, and before going murmured to Thierry that he was leaving him in good hands. I took him straight to the bar, where I bought him a beer and tried to explain in my rudimentary French what I needed from him, though he really didn't inspire me with confidence: Thierry looked too old, even sickly, somehow, and I assumed he was lying when he said he was only fifty-six. His was the most wrinkled black face I had ever seen, he was almost completely bald, and the little hair he still had didn't amount to more than a few clumps of kinky white scattered behind his ears and at the nape of his neck. Since he was missing some teeth, the tip of his tongue, an immensely pale tongue, protruded whenever he talked, and I concluded that in the field at midnight, setting out on the difficult treks of an expedition, this man would not be of much use to me.

He was wearing a purple shirt that day, and it occurred to me that I could use it to show him the exact color of the frog I was looking for. I took a piece of paper and drew it for him, exactly as Vaughan Patterson had drawn it for me in the restaurant in Nashville. Thierry sat looking at the sketch; he spent a long while deep in thought, and I assumed it was just a trick to gain time. Finally he asked for the pencil, held the sketch on his thighs, and drew a circle around the creature's eye, then darkened the lower half of the circle so that it would contrast with the upper half, and finally added a dot at the tip of its snout. He handed back the drawing and told me that the upper arc was silvery, the lower one light brown, and the tip of the snout yellow or grayish-yellow.

I nodded in silence, not taking my eyes off the sketch; now I was the one trying to gain a few moments. When I looked at Thierry, I saw that he was smiling: The last time he had seen the *grenouille du sang,* almost forty years ago, it was not on the Mont des Enfants Perdus. Then he stopped, his face lit up as it always did when he was about to tell one of his stories—though there was no way I could know this at the time—and he recalled every detail of the mission that had brought him to the spot where he saw the frog.

"Do you know what I was looking for on Casetaches?"

I shook my head while I counted out the money for his advance: Thierry had said he needed an advance before he started work.

"I was looking for a woman, sir."

I handed him the money and sat listening to him for over two hours. His observations concerning the frog were meant only to enrich the main story, which is to say, the tale of a bored tourist, an unfortunate German woman who was either miserably unhappy, or crazy, and had gone to live in a cave.

At that time he had already been working a few months for another frog hunter, "a man like you," he said, who had arranged to meet him in the very same hotel (the Oloffson bar, he remembered, had a green piano back then; an old man, one of the guests, came down to the bar with his pet snake around his shoulders; a half-naked woman named June sang there, sitting on the green piano), and who agreed to hire him, just see how similar we were, only after drawing a couple of toads on a little slate and asking if he could recognize them.

Jasper Wilbur, whom Thierry had nicknamed "Papa Crapaud," taught him how to tell one frog from the other according to voice, color, and size, their dorsal stripes or the spots on their bellies. He showed him how to trap the animals without bruising them too much, how to measure them and find out if there was a membrane between their toes, if they had a tongue, or happened to be carrying eggs. As he continued to relate the details of his apprenticeship, I recalled that Wilbur, who was also an Australian, had been the teacher and friend of old man Patterson, and I took it as a good omen that after so much time the circle was closing at precisely this spot—with me, and the same guide grown old, and perhaps the same frogs.

My mother always said you had to look at life as if it were the suspicious start of a crime: tying up loose ends, finding clues, following the trail coldly, as if it didn't even concern you. According to her, nothing that happened was accidental, and it was better to accept this before the suspect fled and the crime was left unsolved. My mother was a painter who knew she was mediocre, and she hated many things, but more than anything else she hated batrachians, which is why she painted them in oils. On the day I told her of my decision to study zoology, shortly before I started college, she fell silent and then ran to her studio. That night she gave me a present, a painting of a midwife toad (*Alytes obstetricans*), an enormous canvas she had kept for many years: She began to paint it when she learned she was pregnant and finished it on the day I was born. From then on she suspected that my life, my entire adult life, would be bound up with those creatures.

Formal work with Thierry was to start two days later, when we would attempt our first expedition to the Mont des Enfants Perdus; in spite of everything, and in order to follow Patterson's instructions, I was determined to go there. Before that, we would stop in Ganthier, a little town at the foot of the mountain, where Thierry had some friends, people who pastured their animals on the slopes or simply went up to cut wood. Since the days when Papa Crapaud had traveled in Haiti, many things had changed in the country, and one of those things was the forest: According to Thierry, not even the trees wanted to grow there, which was why the sides of the mountain looked so bare from down below. We would ask the people in Ganthier if by any chance they had seen the *grenouille du sang*. It would be a hard thing for them to admit, nobody wanted to acknowledge the shame of their bad fortune in front of a stranger, but Thierry assured me he would be able to ask the question without arousing suspicion or fear.

We said our good-byes at the door of the hotel. It was November, and an indefinable stench came from the street, something like sea air, but mixed with the stink of sweat, the sweat of nobody in particular, of passersby, of the women squatting everywhere trying to sell their wares, usually vegetables and hats, the sweat of the waiters as well as my own: In Haiti my perspiration had turned rank, almost thick, and when it dried, it stiffened my shirt. Several times a day I found myself sniffing under my arms; I was intrigued by the odor, my own unfamiliar odor like the odor in a dream. Inhaling that intense, personal, unexpected smell gratified a part of me I can't define, it stimulated my senses, I thought it made me more attractive.

Thierry took out a handkerchief the same color as his shirt, the exact color of the *Eleutherodactylus sanguineus*, a dirty handkerchief that he used to wipe his perspiring bald head and the little beads of sweat around his lips. He looked at me, I suppose with some tenderness, and said I reminded him too much of his Papa Crapaud, a good man who did not deserve the great misfortune he'd had to suffer.

I knew that Jasper Wilbur was buried in Haiti, but I avoided the trap of asking what misfortune that was, or how he had died, or in what shabby cemetery he lay buried. Thierry waited in vain for the question, then began walking down the street, through the crowd, his head high, inexplicably agile, even robust: The light of the world gave him that vitality.

It had to be the light.

Over the past thirteen years, four species of frogs have disappeared from the forests of Queensland, Australia, among them *Taudactylus diurnus* and *Rheobatrachus silus*.

Taudactylus diurnus was seen for the last time in Connondale Ranges, early in 1979.

The last moribund specimen of *Rheobatrachus silus* was found in 1981.

Rheobactrachus silus was first described in May 1973. In the same year, the herpetologist Chris Corben discovered that this was the only animal in the world to develop embryos in its stomach. Its stomach, however, did not differ from that of other species except for the fact that when it contained embryos, the walls grew thinner and production of hydrochloric acid ceased.

Scientists were attempting to investigate the suppression of acids as a possible treatment for gastric diseases in humans.

No one ever discovered how the tadpoles obtained oxygen or excreted their wastes.

Now no one ever will.

XOX FOUR XOX

Heart

By this time my mother had died. My brother Etienne had moved to Côteaux to work in his father-in-law's carpentry shop. My sister Yoyotte still lived in Bombardopolis and was cooking at the food stand owned by her godmother, Yoyotte Placide, who was now a very old woman.

We had just sat down at the table. Jean Pierre, my twin brother, was peeling a banana; Paul, the youngest of my mother's brood, was humming a tune from Martinique; Julien, Frou-Frou's son, was playing *macoute perdu* with the knives and forks and spoons; it was his favorite game. Frou-Frou was there too, she had moved into our house when my mother died; just then she was arguing with Carmelite because the rice hadn't been cooked enough. Then we heard my father's voice; we weren't expecting him because he worked nights with his crew, but we saw him come in and we were silent. He ordered the table cleared and told the women to prepare coffee, then he told Paul to wait outside. Since he didn't call us by name, and never had, he fixed his eyes on the spot where Jean

Pierre and I were sitting next to each other, looked at Jean Pierre, and told him to go out too. He didn't have to say a word to Julien: As if it were part of his game, he ran to the door, shot at us with his wooden gun, and disappeared.

I was the only one left in the room, and my father sat down beside me, I was the one he wanted to talk to; he said, "You stay."

We didn't know yet that he had come home with two men. One was a foreigner from the land of the Germans, the other was a Haitian who worked at a hotel in Port-au-Prince and could speak English; the German had hired him to help him talk to my father: What he wanted was for my father to find his wife.

She had been seen the day before in Jérémie. The men in my father's crew saw her, the hunters I've been telling you about; they worked till dawn, just waiting for a beast to appear, so when they saw her they followed her for a while—the woman was staggering around the village—and then let her go on her way when they realized she was out of her mind. You can't imagine how many women go out of their minds as soon as they set foot in Haiti, decent women who come for a little sun and end up on the burros with twisted hooves that go up to the Citadelle. It's the worst mistake they can make, because after that, I don't know why, they come back deranged, their clothes all dirty and their eyes popping out of their heads; that's how they wander around the country, it makes you sick to see them. If they brought a husband with them, the husband drags them back to the ship or plane they came on. If they're alone, and some of them are, the police pick them up and put them in an insane asylum. Then the doctors get word to their families and before you know it, a brother, a father, a son shows up, it's always a man who comes for them, and they're handed over to that man.

That night my father told me what he knew: The woman had passed through Jérémie, but instead of staying on the beach or walking toward Bonbon, a quiet little village, she stopped a truck going to Dame-Marie and asked the driver to take her there, she offered him money and the man gave her a ride. When they were halfway to Dame-Marie, just as they were passing Casetaches Hill, she yelled that she was getting out. The man warned her it wasn't a good place for a lady by herself; she didn't answer but got out anyway and headed right for the woods.

I know Casetaches, sir, like the palm of my hand. When I lived in Jérémie, I'd go up there twice a week. Papa Crapaud came with me, I helped him collect his frogs and also set traps to catch mongooses; I slit them open to see if they'd eaten a toad, and if they had, Papa Crapaud had to know about it.

When I didn't go with him, I went up with Carmelite, who had grown into a beautiful girl. Frou-Frou knew we went there together and didn't seem to care; my father also knew and cared even less. I think deep down he envied me, he would have liked to go somewhere with his own stepdaughter, but by this time he was old, he could put up with it.

In those days Casetaches had seven caves (today there are only five left), and I knew the inside of all of them, which is why my father decided I should be the one to look for the woman: The German was going to pay in advance; by now you know I like to be paid in advance. My one condition was that my brother Paul should go with me. I got along better with Jean Pierre, but his being lame was bound to hold me back. As soon as I said that, my father became very serious and slammed his hand down on the table: This was a job a man should do by himself; if he had told my brothers not to interfere, who was I to ask for a helper?

I opened my mouth to explain that it wasn't a good idea to climb the hill alone, but my father opened his eyes wide and looked at me in a way that made me bow my head:

"If you don't have the balls to do it, say so now and I'll find somebody else."

I didn't say anything, I mean, in a very quiet voice I said I was ready to go.

That night the German slept in our house; the one little hotel in Jérémie was closed and Frou-Frou told Carmelite to fix up a cot for him. He was a man our father's age, his hands were covered with spots and he was always looking at his watch. The Haitian who had come with him also slept under our roof. Carmelite gave him a blanket because we didn't have another cot, and when he stood there holding it, not knowing what to do, Frou-Frou came over right away, scolded her daughter for being so impolite, took the blanket, and spread it on the floor. The man lay down and Frou-Frou brought him coffee; the German didn't want anything to drink; he wrapped himself in the blanket we had given him and just stared at the ceiling until we turned off the light.

Before he went out again with his crew, my father told Frou-Frou to fix a knapsack for me with water, food, rum, and an oilskin in case it rained at night. And he told her to put in a rope for tying up the lost woman. On her own, Frou-Frou packed some cigarettes, and finally I put in a jar with alcohol in case I saw a good frog on Casetaches for Papa Crapaud, who had gone to the island of Guadeloupe to look for frogs in that country.

The next morning Frou-Frou pulled at my shirt to wake me. I had slept with my clothes on, so I took the knapsack, turned on my flashlight, and crept out very slow and quiet so I wouldn't disturb the others. When I passed the German's cot, the light shined for a second on his face and I saw that his eyes were still open, still staring at the ceiling. The blanket that Frou-Frou had spread for the other man was on the floor, but he wasn't on it; I thought he must have grown tired of the hard floor and found some other place to sleep.

I began to walk toward the square. My father told me to get on the first truck leaving for Dame-Marie and to get out at the place where the woman got out. We didn't know how long it would take to find her, so we agreed that whether or not I found her I'd go back to the road the next night and they'd be waiting for me in a car: the German, my father, and the man who was helping them understand each other.

The sun was already high when I jumped off the truck. Between the road and Casetaches there's a long stretch without any trees, and you think you're never going to get to the hill. But you get there soon enough if instead of looking into the distance while you walk you keep your eyes on the ground; very soon you come to a line of low bushes they call *oeuf de poule*, and from that point on you can say you've reached the hill.

My father taught me that before you go onto a mountain you have to ask permission; you ask the *loas*, the "mysteries" who rule this land. That was another of his old ways. Well, that day I asked for the right to go up, I didn't always remember to do it, I crossed myself as soon as the shadow of the first bushes fell across my face, I closed my eyes and whispered, "Baron Samedi, Baron-la-Croix, Papa Lokó, I ask permission to go on the mountain"; I pushed aside the bushes a little and prayed to all the *loas*, all of them, to please open the way for me.

I spent the rest of the morning and most of the afternoon looking for tracks. My father, who was the best tracker in his crew, had taught me how to find the trail of humans, which is different and dirtier than the trail of animals. Since it wasn't a good idea for the woman to see me before I saw her, I covered my hat with some branches and kept putting more over my pack whenever they fell off. Maybe I'd find her dead: She'd spent two days on the mountain, exposed to the bites of *cul-rouge* spiders, or purple scorpions. If she was too crazy she probably didn't have water to drink; you have to be in your right mind to find water on Casetaches.

By nightfall there was no sign of the woman, not even her damn shadow. I sat down to rest on a rock and covered myself with the oilskin because it had started to rain, and I opened the bottle of rum that Frou-Frou had put in my knapsack and began to think about the caves that were not too far away, about which one would be best for spending the night. That's what I was doing when I heard the song of the *grenouille du sang*; this creature's call isn't an ordinary one, it's a kind of *glug-glug-glug*, like the sound of a great bubble coming up from deep inside.

My skin crawled. The last time I heard it I was a boy, and the very next day I got the fever and saw death coming for me: a brown devil pig with three front legs, and I told my father about it and to comfort me he brought me that fruit like a young girl's flesh. Nobody in my family, not one of us, ever liked to hear the call of this frog. I swear I began to tremble, something in the night was wrong, and I decided to look for the animal and make it be quiet. Papa Crapaud had taught me not to become confused, he had warned me that sometimes when you hear the call in one place it means that the frog is somewhere else. They do it to throw lizards off the track, and rats, and who knows, maybe to throw men off the track too.

I took off the oilskin and the rain ran down my face. I moved some leaves aside and shined the light on the ground and into the hollows of trees. The frog stopped singing as soon as it knew it was being hunted; I turned off the light so it would start to sing again, and then, in the darkness, I saw its eyes, I mean, the two silvery half-moons, moving in front of me. I could have squashed it if I wanted to, or put it in the jar and kept it for Papa Crapaud, who would have given anything to see it, but it occurred to me that maybe bad luck came with the grenouille du sang because everybody killed it. If I let it live, maybe it would go to the loas, who are its natural masters, and quiet them by telling them how well I had treated it.

I moved a little closer and shined the light right on it to blind it: It was hiding under a rock, but I could see that it was as red as a fruit, as red as the heart of an animal. Then the rain started to pour down and it moved, it left its shelter and came out into the rain; with the gleam of the water, it seemed to me that yes, it did look like it was covered in blood, it made you happy to see it, and it made you afraid.

I was about to go even closer when it leaped away and disappeared, that's when I turned off the flashlight and felt like crying. I was still very young and so I thought about my dead mother, I prayed to her spirit to protect me. While I was praying I heard the sound of footsteps; somebody was walking in a circle around me.

I threw myself to the ground—my father always said the best thing to do when you're surrounded is to move like that, hugging the ground—but I didn't have time to move because my hand brushed something in the darkness, something soft and clammy, and I pretended it was the frog, the frog again, I told myself it was a frog so I wouldn't tell myself the truth: that the thing I touched was the instep of a foot, the living foot of a human being. I dug in my nails and turned on the flashlight: The woman stood there, naked, her whole body streaming water and blood, water from the rain and blood from who knows where. I tried to stand and felt a blow on my back, I looked up and she struck again, she was hitting me with a branch from the *arbre au diable*, and the black thorns on the branch, and they're very poisonous, cut into my cheek, one came close to my eye and for a minute everything went black and I thought she had torn out my eye.

You've probably noticed that lunatics, no matter how stupid and weak they seem, always have more strength than sane people. Well, she had that strength and she hit me a lot of times before I could grab the branch away from her. Then it was my turn: I swung at her, just once, but hard, I hit her across the back and she fell facedown

and began kicking; I put my foot on the back of her neck,
then I used my knees to hold her down, that was the only
way I could tie her hands. I could feel her trembling, I
don't know if it was from cold or rage. I made her stand
up and pushed her to force her to walk, I said if she
didn't, I'd drag her along the ground into the cave. She
wasn't all that crazy because she obeyed, and we both
walked for a long time until we came to the Rat Cave,
that was the name I gave the place when I was a little boy.

Instead of feeling satisfied because the next day I
would collect the rest of the money, I was very confused, I
wondered how any man could go to so much trouble to
hunt down a woman as homely as this one, a woman who
didn't even seem like a woman. I stared at her out of
curiosity: I never did like white women, but this one was
so skinny she hardly had any breasts, seeing her naked was
like looking at my little brother Paul, my own brother in
white and blonde, though you couldn't really say she had
much hair. And a woman should have a bush of hair
between her legs and under her arms, and another on her
head. That's what my father always said: "A female without those three bushes is a female you can't trust."

I tried to imagine the face he'd make when he found
out that the woman on Casetaches had hair so short you
could see her skull, just a few strands of cornsilk under
her arms, and between her legs it was shaved, believe me
when I tell you, she had taken a razor to it, what kind of
woman does something like that? I made her drink some
rum so she wouldn't die on me before I got her back to
her husband. I said that her husband was looking for her
and was going to pay a lot of money to see her again and
that ought to make her happy because not every husband

sent people to look for a wife when she got crazy and ran away. She didn't understand the words from my mouth, but I know she was starting to understand the ones in my thoughts.

It was almost dawn when she began to cough. I threw the oilskin over her shoulders, and she fell asleep. That's when I heard her voice for the first time. She talked in a very quiet voice, like she was talking to her dead, and even though I couldn't understand the words in her mouth either, one by one I started to understand the ones in her heart. To tell the truth, I felt sorry for her then, and I closed my eyes to bring on sleep; all I wanted was for day to break and then night to fall so I could take her back down the mountain.

It was almost midday when I woke up. The woman's eyes were open very wide and she had managed to shrug off the oilskin. It was hot inside the cave. I put a piece of cassava bread in her mouth and she spit it out, then I forced her to drink a mouthful of water with sugar. She couldn't die, I told her, not till we got off the mountain. She didn't say a word, she didn't even groan when I poured a little rum into an open wound on her head, she must have cut it on a tree trunk. I told her I was doing it for her own good: We had a long time to wait before it got dark and we could go back to the village, and the *cul-rouge* spiders like the taste of blood. That place was full of *cul-rouges*, and to prove it to her, I found one of the big ones and held it up in front of her. She didn't make a face, she didn't scream, she didn't seem afraid of it. Just the opposite. She brought her face up close and touched the spider's belly with her nose, its legs brushed against her mouth, she thought that was funny and began to laugh.

Then I dropped the creature and it scurried back to its corner.

I left the cave and ate the dried meat that Frou-Frou had packed for me, then I walked around, I didn't like being near that woman, I didn't want to see her again until it was time for us to go down. In those days the mountain had more trees than it does now: Down below was the *oeuf de poule*, but the *bois immortel*, the *brucal*, the *mancenillier* all grew up on the slopes, all of them were good for the same thing: for getting poison.

We used poison for fishing, we threw it in the water, over the fish, and stunned them so we could pull them out. The juice of the *mancenillier* hurt people's skin, and the *pwazon rat* in my father's crew often climbed up to collect it, along with the leaves of the *bois cacá* and the bark of the *bois marbre*. They fed the leaves to horses to make them shed their manes and tails; if you fed a single leaf to a woman, she lost all her hair, those three bushes my father liked so much. The bark of the *bois marbre* was burned next to the hiding places of beasts they were tracking, then the beasts came out for air, stumbled out because the smoke of the *marbre* clouds the eyes, and then they were caught.

I walked the countryside till it grew dark. I spent the time catching lizards for Papa Crapaud. Not ordinary lizards, but blind white lizards that you almost never saw; I found a nest of them and pulled them out by the tail, one by one, noticing the stripe on their side, a little green line that didn't always end at the same spot. Papa Crapaud said it was important to check how many lizards had the little green line ending at their bellies and how many had it going farther back, right back to where their toes started. All of this had to be written down before they were put into alcohol, because the alcohol cooked them and those lizards had such white skin they turned almost transparent. I didn't have paper and pencil that day, but on the little slate of my mind—so much smaller than the slate Papa Crapaud always carried with him—I made a note that on five of the creatures the stripe ended at their middles; it ended at their toes on only two.

I went back to the cave and saw that the woman had fallen asleep. I woke her, I tied the oilskin around her waist, and we set out. She had an awful smell, something like the odor of the *tulipe du mort*, I don't know if you've seen that flower: It has a black bloom about this size, and when you squeeze it, out spurts a stinking juice. Well, that's just what she smelled like. Maybe it was the only thing she could find to drink while she was wandering around the mountain, and now she was sweating out the deadly juice: You'd have to be thirstier than a hanged man to swallow the bile of that flower.

She fell a few times, or maybe she just pretended to fall. I helped her up and bit my tongue so I wouldn't lose my temper. I tried to think about the money I was earning, I figured out how much I would spend on one thing, how much on another, and in my mind I subtracted the percentage my father would take.

Once when the woman fell, I heard the *glug-glug-glug* of the *grenouille du sang* again, I couldn't tell if it was the same frog but I thought it was, the same one and it was following us. By this time we were pretty close to the road and it worried me that I didn't see a light. I had arranged with my father that they'd leave the headlights on so I could find them, I began to ask myself what would happen if nobody came to pick us up that night, what I would do then with this white woman who was naked and bleeding. She pulled at me and said a few words, she stopped and went on talking, not noticing that I didn't understand, then she screamed something and threw herself to the ground. She knew I was taking her to her husband and she didn't want to go back. I tried to make her stand up and she bit my hand, with the same hand I slapped her face, and her head rocked from side to side because I kept hitting her. It scared me to think they had abandoned us.

Then I decided the best thing was to wait right there, so I rested against some bushes, turned off the flashlight, and in the darkness I listened to the woman breathing and tried to believe this was the way she always breathed, like she was hurling her soul out of her mouth. After a time the two headlights flashed on and off and then on again: That was the signal and I knew my father was down below, I never felt so happy to know he was nearby. I took the woman by the arm and she got up without a struggle. It seems she had changed her mind, she had resigned herself or forgotten that she didn't want to resign herself: Then she walked so fast the oilskin slipped off her body and I couldn't cover her again.

Her husband was waiting for us at the side of the road; I went up to him and gave his wife back to him. My father and the Haitian who helped them understand each other had stayed inside the car and they called to me to come inside too. I heard the husband talking very softly and then he began to raise his voice, the night was dark and I shined my flashlight on them: The woman still had her hands tied but suddenly she spit at him, she wanted to spit in his face but the man moved and the spittle landed on his chest; my father cursed and I turned off the light. I climbed into the car without saying a word, nobody said anything to me either, and then I heard shouts again, they were both shouting but you also heard the sound of blows, and I thought about asking my father to tell the husband not to hit his wife too hard because she could die. But my father cursed again and then I couldn't say anything.

The husband opened the door on my side, I changed my seat right away, and he threw in his wife like a man throwing in a bundle; she moaned very quietly, and when we were on our way she vomited, I smelled blood and my shoes were covered with hot liquid. Later she moaned again, and from time to time a putrid bubble boiled up from deep in her throat, it was like the song of the frog.

When we reached Jérémie, the German said something to the Haitian who was traveling with him, and the Haitian asked us where we wanted to go. My father told him to take us to the port, and I asked for the rest of my money but nobody answered me and I didn't open my mouth again.

Some light came in from the streets and I could see the woman's face, she had passed out or she was dead, her nose was bloody and there was dried blood on one ear.

The car stopped across from the sea, and only the Haitian from Port-au-Prince said good-bye to us; the German looked at his watch and then turned around to look at the collapsed bundle that was his wife. My father and I got out and then the tires squealed and we saw them drive off toward Roseaux.

We walked slowly toward our house, my father began to smoke, and on the way he stopped, took out a roll of bills, and gave them to me. There were some dollars in

among the *gourdes;* I didn't count them in front of him, I
wasn't brave enough to do that. Frou-Frou was serving
dinner, Carmelite helped her set out the plates, and Julien,
my father's youngest son, was playing another game of
macoute perdu. I didn't see Paul, but I heard him in the bathroom singing the song he always sang:

> *Toc-toc qui est-ce qui*
> *frappe a mon porte?*
> *C'est moi doudou,*
> *c'est moi l'amour.*

I took out the jars with the lizards I had hunted for
Papa Crapaud, arranged them in front of my bed, and
Carmelite came right away to see them. Julien left off his
game and came too, skipping, pushing to get a better view.
Then Frou-Frou, with my father behind her, and they
both started to laugh, my father laughing and laughing
like he was hearing a very funny joke.

Finally everybody calmed down and Frou-Frou served
the soup, I got a whiff of it and looked at my shoes, I
hadn't remembered until then that they were dirty. That
was the signal for my guts to turn over, a tangle of worms
came up into my mouth and I hardly had time to run out
of the house and spit it onto the ground, with as much
difficulty and grief as if I was spitting out my own heart.

✕✦✕ FIVE ✕✦✕

Birds You Don't Know

It's no animal: these are human bones."

Thierry continued digging through the mound and after a time found what he was looking for: a brownish skull. From my vantage point I watched him dust off his treasure, hold it up with one hand, inspect the empty sockets and the meager cavity of the mouth.

"They broke his teeth," he added, "and the jawbone was fractured from underneath."

He brought over the skull and placed it in front of me, but I didn't look at it right away; I went on with the task of identifying the jars. We had spent three days and nights camped on the Mont des Enfants Perdus, and all I had managed to catch was a handful of specimens of *Bufo gurgulio*, a little blue-bellied toad whose call I had taped the same night Thierry talked about his memories, the night I thought of Martha again and my predicted death by fire.

"There are bones enough for seven bodies. Seven at least."

He said this slowly, as if relishing his own calculations,

but underneath he was terrified; I knew because of his hands, he could barely control the tremor in his fingers. Initially, when we discovered the first remains, I said they must be an animal's, I couldn't conceive of anything else. I tried to convince him, I wanted to get him away from the place, but he only showed me an open rib cage. His triumph was complete when he finally pulled out the skull.

"The police will have to be notified," I admitted, not showing too much alarm. "Go down to Ganthier and tell them." He didn't reply but went back to the mound and resumed his search. I picked up the skull with two fingers and examined the inside; it still smelled of rotting flesh, and bits of tissue clung to the gums. I looked at the broken bone, discovered another fracture behind the left ear, then put it down with the jars containing the preserved toads and went over to Thierry. I watched in silence as he dug through the earth, stood beside him until he found a second skull.

"There must be seven of them," he said again, "I swear to God."

I grabbed his arm and forced him to drop his find.

"You shouldn't take out any more. Go down to the village and let them know."

"This is all the knowing we need," he grumbled, and now his voice was different, now it was hollow. "We both have to go down."

I pretended I hadn't heard and took the map we had drawn last night from my pocket.

"I still have to comb through this area behind the dry woods."

"Down, we have to go down," he insisted, his head bowed. "Can't you see we're bothering them?"

I went back to the jars and put them away in my knapsack. The skull was by itself, apprehensive and defenseless in the weeds, and I covered it with a handkerchief and placed it under a tree.

"If we stay here tonight," Thierry whispered, "we're going to end up in a bone pile too."

He pointed at the mound that had been disturbed; swarms of flies had begun to gather. He seemed sincere and yet I felt obliged to doubt, to deny the absurd danger that threatened to interfere with my work, to forget everything except the one thing that had brought me to the mountain: Nothing very serious can happen to a man when all he looks for, all he wants, is a harmless little frog.

"Let's go back to camp," I said to Thierry, "then we'll see."

"The mountain is occupied," he said emphatically, looking toward the trees, "they told me in Ganthier."

I finished adjusting the knapsack and saw that he had begun to pray, muttering invocations with his fists clenched and his face pressed into the ground. I thought it was a passing fear, that as soon as he finished all his "Our Fathers" he'd walk with me to the place where we had set up camp, and we'd light a big fire, heat some cans of food, and eat outdoors, as we had for the past three nights, listening to the news on the radio.

I decided to be patient, a researcher must expect things like this; I learned that years ago when I was studying the reproductive habits of the *Pipa pipa*. In Suriname I had a guide much older than Thierry, a grave, melancholy man who begged the toad's pardon before he caught it. He stayed with me to the end, but twice I had to join him in a ritual to appease the demons.

Thierry raised his head and I saw the panic that had concentrated there, hanging like a lead weight between his eyebrows.

"We have to go down while we still can"—his forehead was covered with sweat—"and at night we won't be able to."

I shook my head and turned my back. I wanted to find a phrase, a single word, that would melt his fear, but he spoke first.

"I'm talking to you from the heart, sir. I know what this mountain is used for, nobody can come up here, not even to look for frogs. You must want to get back home safe and sound, you must want to see your children, you have children, don't you?"

I thought that even if we pushed ourselves we wouldn't reach camp in less than two hours. I looked at my watch; it was a quarter to five and I estimated we'd be there by nightfall. It would be easier to persuade him in camp.

"I had some," Thierry said, "but they all died. The first one died right after he was born, the rest were older."

I recalled that the night before I left, Martha had mentioned again that Haiti wasn't a safe place. We had supper at home, and I avoided looking at her: I knew she didn't care about my safety, she was trying to frighten me in a way that didn't suit her—not very skillful and with a good deal of rage, moved by a free-floating rancor that went back and forth across the table. I didn't wait to finish my soup; I dipped my spoon and instead of bringing it up to my mouth, I spilled its contents on the tablecloth, next to her plate, and then I threw it down. Martha closed her eyes and didn't say another word to me, not even good-bye.

"When I lost my first child," Thierry said with a sigh, "I thought a lot about my father. He always had a very difficult trade."

Thierry's father had been a wary man who avoided speaking the names of his children. My own father and Martha never got along. It was a powerful antipathy, born practically out of nothing, a war with no beginning, always present: an electric, secret hatred. You could see it even in the way they greeted one another, in the effort each of them made not to refer to the other.

"Now I'm going to tell you what a *pwazon rat* is. My father was one."

We were walking so quickly that Thierry's words came out in a rush; many of them I couldn't understand, they were extinguished like sparks as soon as they burst from his lips. Sometimes he paused to catch his breath and take a swallow of water, and after the water a swallow of the white liquor they call *clairin* in Haiti; sometimes he stopped to look at me, he would say something dirty or repugnant and search my face to see my reaction.

"My father liked to risk his skin. I knew they might kill him one day, so I often went with him and was by his side on his last hunts."

When he finished his story, Thierry asked if my father also hunted frogs. I answered no, he had spent his life selling cars, he was the best salesman and eventually had his own business. But now he was old, he had retired and now he did strange work, dangerous too, in a way.

"He raises birds," I said.

"Chickens?"

"No, Thierry, birds you don't know. They can kill a man with one kick."

The story intrigued him, but just then the camp came into view and he raised his arms:

"They were here, I can smell them."

The tent had disappeared, and all that was left of the sleeping bags were some shreds scattered around a tree. Jars lay broken on the ground, and singed journals and notebooks, empty cans, rumpled clothes were tossed everywhere. The most recent issue of *Froglog*, a monthly bulletin of data concerning the decline in amphibians, lay on a stone, covered with a pile of shit.

"We have to go down," Thierry repeated. "We're bothering them on this mountain."

I asked who it was we were bothering, but he raised a finger to his lips and told me to be quiet. He took a nylon bag from his knapsack and began to pick up the unbroken jars. I broke off a branch and tried to save part of the bulletin: The August *Froglog* included an article of mine with a photograph of the *Rana pipiens*, which had disappeared in Canada. The photo and the title of my article could not be seen under the stain left by the turds. I didn't try to save anything else.

"If we leave now," Thierry insisted, "they won't kill us. They could have done it a while ago."·

I was so stunned I accepted his words as valid. In this elemental light of terror and survival, it struck me as almost natural that they would destroy our camp and intimidate us into leaving the mountain; natural that they would spare our lives, give us some time, a last chance, a little reprieve.

"We'll have to walk in the dark," he said, "but it doesn't matter, I've done it lots of times."

I had no arguments left, I didn't even have a place to

sit and write. I turned on my flashlight and covered my face with insect repellent; I offered some to Thierry but he refused: The bugs knew him by now, years ago they had bitten him plenty and now they left his hide alone. He laughed as he spoke, the first time I had seen him laugh in a long time. That gave me enough confidence and courage to ask again who was throwing us out, who we were bothering.

"The *attachés* of Cito Francisque," he whispered in my ear, "they use this mountain to store their shipments and kill troublemakers. They don't want any stranger in the area, nobody looking for frogs or any other animal."

Night had fallen when we began the descent. Thierry went first, moving aside branches, orienting himself by the placement of the trees: It was very overcast and we couldn't see the sky. I didn't open my mouth, but on two or three occasions he turned around and ordered me to be quiet; later I stumbled and fell to my knees, I cursed and he came back and proposed a short rest. That was when we drank the last mouthfuls from our canteens, and he turned off his flashlight and spoke to me in the darkness:

"They're following us."

The air was very heavy, and in the distance I made out the call of other specimens of *Bufo gurgulio*; it was their mating season and the males were desperate to consummate the embrace, the interminable, delicious amplexus that would return them to silence. Apparently there were no longer enough females. Some extinctions begin this way, first the females disappear, vanish with their wombs full. Where do they go, what is it they fear, why the hell do they run away? Thierry turned on his flashlight again, and I had to look at the horror on his face, a ruined mask, another half-eaten skull barely rescued from the living bone pile of the night.

"When we get to Ganthier, if we ever get there, you'll tell me about the birds your father raises."

I felt a wave of resentment; I was irritated by his attitude, the paternalistic way he allowed himself to change the subject. I decided I'd let him go as soon as we reached safety. I reached out my hand and grabbed his shirt.

"What is it they want, do they want money?"

"Not yours," Thierry said curtly. "You don't have enough."

He freed himself with a brusque movement, and at that moment terror overwhelmed me. It had begun to rain and he disappeared behind some bushes. I made an effort not to call out, I raised my own flashlight and held it high as I walked forward. That was when I heard whispers, the thin sound of voices; the rain grew heavier and I resigned myself to the idea of death. A wet, remote death on a mountain of lost children and elusive frogs. The miserable death of a man who doesn't know who is pursuing him or why they attack him. Perhaps that was the only fire I would see, the absurd flames in which the Tibetan astrologer had seen me burning.

I felt drunk, as if I were going to fall. I heard the whispers again, and firm steps walking around me, then a hand pressed against my back: It was Thierry.

"They want to be sure we're going," he said.

It was hard for me to walk, but much harder to think, to connect facts, to draw any conclusions. I was at the mercy of a nature complicit with that steep section of slope, and I was at the mercy of my pursuers, and it all somehow included Thierry himself.

An hour later we finally saw the lights of Ganthier. I think we both felt relieved, and he began to whisper what might have been another prayer.

"So you didn't hear anything?" was the first thing he asked when he finished his supplication.

"I heard the voices," I said. "What else was I supposed to hear?"

In Ganthier we took refuge in the house of the man who was taking care of the car, a tomato-red Renault I had rented in Port-au-Prince. They offered us cornmeal stew, and Thierry bought two bottles of liquor. At midnight we lay down on the pounded-earth floor, slept for two or three hours, and at dawn the owner of the house called us: We ought to leave the village at first light.

We drove back in silence, and just before Port-au-Prince, Thierry signaled for me to stop beside an enormous garbage dump behind which, he declared, he lived with his brother Jean Pierre. He wanted me to go there with him but I refused. He climbed out slowly, and immediately put his face up to the window:

"What time do you want to see me tomorrow?"

I was going to tell him I didn't need him anymore; I suppose he saw it on my face because he shook his head, got back in the car, and looked straight ahead, toward the place where a few children were playing with some kind of half-dead squirrel.

"Last night I heard the *grenouille du sang.*"

I preferred to think he was lying; I tried to show him I knew he was lying. I looked at him, smiled, and asked just when he had heard it.

"When I went behind the bushes, remember? I heard it call twice, I thought you heard it too."

"You should have said so then." My voice was distant, as if I really didn't care. "We'll talk later . . . ".

"I swear by the memory of my children that I heard it."

I slammed my hand against the steering wheel and he understood that I was ordering him to go away; he bolted out of the car and muttered some kind of excuse, at least that's what I thought it was. One of the children tossed the squirrel into the air. I saw it fall a few meters in front of the car and decided to put an end to its suffering. I accelerated and only felt a slight bump as the tire flattened the body.

I didn't look back, but I heard the shouts. The children were shouting threats at me.

During the winter of 1990, the unexplained deaths of millions of frogs occurred in various ponds in northern Switzerland.

According to reports furnished by KARCH (Commission for the Protection of Amphibians and Reptiles), the *Rana temporaria* was the species most affected.

Due to the fact that nothing like it had occurred before, at least not in that region, and not in winter, the Swiss authorities ordered an investigation. Among the conclusions cited were poor oxygenation of the water, as well as other polluting factors. It was pointed out, however, that these factors by themselves could not explain the large number of dead frogs.

For many biologists, the sudden decline of the *Rana temporaria* remains shrouded in mystery.

SIX

The Hunt

Except when they decided to go into the sea, to the great satisfaction of sharks and carrion-eating fish, the wandering packs of the dead usually took shelter on the slopes of Chilotte. That was when the cattle owners, who feared their vengeance, would hire the *pwazon rats*, and that was when the *pwazon rats* would organize into crews and go out to hunt them.

No one ever knew how they found their way, but sooner or later they all came to Chilotte, the ones running from the Savannah Zombie and those fleeing Piton Mango. And even those who managed to escape from the sleeping hordes of the Grande Colline, on the other side of the Gulf, sooner or later came to this mountain.

Bombardopolis was almost at the foot of Chilotte—it's still there, but more in memory—and in those days it was not unusual to see the living dead cross the town at any hour, so tormented by the sun and so bitten by insects they hardly felt the stones, the children threw stones at them and they didn't know how to dodge them, they slipped and fell, they got up and in a little while they fell again, their eyes fixed on the bare hill.

Filling the doorways of Petit Paradis, which was the name of Yoyotte Placide's food stand, the *pwazon rats* would watch them pass but never tried to stop them. That's what the mountain was for, and it was there, at night and with no witnesses, where they rounded them up, roped them like iguanas, and tied them, like iguanas, to branches.

Then they checked to see if perhaps there were any among them who could be returned to their packs, but they almost never could return any of them because by the time they got to Chilotte most had spent days and days wandering the coast, rolling around in the poisonous shade of the black mangroves, licking the salt that crusted the foliage. It was the salt that woke them, and when they woke they saw themselves as they really were, they remembered what they had been, they were desperate to be that again. Then they went into a rage: They started in kicking, they started in biting, they started in scratching, and since they couldn't even be dragged back to the village, the hunters just pulled off that little piece at the back of the neck where they had the mark of their pack. In exchange for that, the cattle owner would give them money.

Finally, they would herd them all together in one cave and leave them with a *pwazon rat* named Gregoire Oreste. Each member of the crew had his job, and Gregoire Oreste's was to finish off the hunt.

The rest of the men who went out with my father were named Moses Dumbo, Divoine Joseph, Achille Fritz, and Tiburon Jérémie. Moses Dumbo, who at the age of eighty-two was the oldest *pwazon rat* in Haiti, swore that at the final moment some of the savannah zombies had the ability to turn into animals: into wandering hogs, drunken mongooses, or the red-crested hens that appeared suddenly, flapping their wings in the middle of the road, but still they grabbed the prey and put them head first into their bags.

At night, sitting next to the fire, old Dumbo kept his eye on the soup, waiting for the first bubble: Meat that raised a lot of foam was not good meat, meat that turned white right away was not good meat. "Living carrion!" he would shout, and he kept on shouting until he convinced them all to throw it out.

When the moon was full, they didn't go out to hunt. And they didn't go out to hunt on Mondays, they're the days of Baron-la-Croix. And it wasn't a good idea to catch the beasts during Holy Week or on the eve of the Day of the Dead. But the most dangerous thing, more dangerous than capturing the prey and not knowing how to cover it—you had to cover its head—was to go out hunting with an open wound or with a disease you had caught from a woman.

That was why, before they left for the field, Divoine Joseph, who was second-in-command, would make them all undress, and he would examine them one by one: He looked into their mouths and pulled their ears, squeezed their foreskins, spread their cheeks, and felt under their balls. Sometimes he would talk quietly to a man and separate him from the group, that meant he had felt a swelling. But when he made a face and pointed toward the door, that meant they were all healthy and now they could get started.

As soon as they began to climb the mountain, the *pwazon rats* avoided calling each other by name and hardly talked among themselves; instead they began to whistle. Whistling drove the packs crazy—my father said it disoriented them—and when he and Divoine Joseph gave some shrill whistles, not even the men in the crew could stand it. Divoine would signal for them to cover their ears, he covered his too, but not my father. My father used his strength and endured, his eyes closed, his ears rigid.

Sometimes, a beast smarter than the rest would walk behind them, follow them as they moved through the countryside, or hide behind a tree when the crew stopped to eat, and if he couldn't find a tree—by that time the trees were beginning to thin out—he would squat like a toad and hide in the weeds. Without paying much attention to him the men would finish eating as calm as you please and then gather round my father, who would draw the hill trails in the ashes and show each man his route. And he would assign them their prey, sometimes two or three or four of them, depending on how many beasts were in the pack.

Up on the slopes you couldn't close your eyes. When it grew dark, my father gave the order to rest a while in the hammocks. Then they could talk, but in whispers; usually the men would smoke, drink a few mouthfuls of *clairin*, and plan what they would do with the money they'd get for the hunt. But by the time they came down from the hill, those plans had faded away, because when they came down they were wrecks, their heads still ringing with the final shrieks. And so they hurried to Môle Saint Nicolas, which was Divoine Joseph's hometown, ran like madmen to the cabaret that belonged to one-armed Tancréde, and fucked the Dominican girls—there were Dominicans from Santo Domingo and Dominicans from

Haiti, the ones from Haiti were called "homegrown Dominicans"—and drank down whole bottles of that purple molasses they call Cayemite liquor. This was the only way they could rip the taste of death from their souls. In a single night they spent half the wages they had earned: One-armed Tancréde knew his business.

If it began to thunder it was a different story, because this upset the packs and the beasts fought among themselves, or just froze wherever they happened to be when the rain started. The *pwazon rats* preferred to work on stormy nights, not because they were more devilish than the devils they came out to hunt—that's what the gossips in Bombardopolis used to say—but because they could do what they had to do with more calm and less danger.

Too bad there was no storm, no thunder, no mercy at all the day my father died. I think now he was too old for that kind of work, being too old for hunting means being too confident.

My father was killed by an old she-devil named Romaine La Prophetesse, an evil woman in life, you can just imagine what she was like in death. In her day she had been a *mambo*, a priestess, a *madame* with a hard heart whose only weakness was her son, a little runt of a man named Sonsón. To take revenge, to see her in a rage, to destroy the little spirit she had left, somebody killed Sonsón. And all she could do was bury him. But then she found out that he had been seen on the Massacre, the river that swells with misfortune, tossing in a little boat from one side to the other, carrying sacks of coal, not even resting at night, her boy was like a beggar.

Any mother would give her life for her child, but Romaine La Prophetesse did more: She gave her death for him. She ordered her helpers to take her down to the dead, she wanted to suffer what Sonsón had suffered. Her funeral was really something, the truth is that nothing like it had ever been seen in Haiti: a person who would go down of her own free will. When they woke her, they fed her *cocombre zombi* paste, and she turned fierce and went straight to the Massacre. But her dear boy was no longer there, she couldn't find him even though she searched both banks, somebody told her he'd been burned, that's why she became such a bitch.

The day she ambushed my father, Romaine La Prophetesse was traveling with her pack along the trails of Chilotte, a pack of savannah zombies as hungry and bloodthirsty as she was. They caught him far from camp, doing his business in some bushes—that was another of his old habits: My father never let anybody see him shit, he said it was the moment of greatest weakness for a man and he would go away from his people to do it.

The men in the crew didn't suspect a thing, they didn't even hear any screams. A *pwazon rat* knows how to defend himself, it's his duty to defend himself with nails and teeth, with a machete, with whatever he needs, but he never screams. A man goes in silence, my father would say, and he goes with his thoughts on his future.

Later, Divoine Joseph and Moses Dumbo found the body. They found it without its skin. Those beasts had flayed him and left him lying in his own shit. Frou-Frou washed him anyway, but afterward she complained that her hands had stuck to his raw flesh, that my father's little veins had wrapped around her fingers like worms. A body without its skin is disgusting, but even so, Frou-Frou dressed him in his shirt.

The whole family gathered for the wake. My brother Jean Pierre was the one who cried the most and my brother Etienne had to fortify him. Three bottles of liquor weren't enough. My sister Yoyotte and her godmother brought the body from Bombardopolis. Old Yoyotte Placide fainted in Frou-Frou's arms: There's nothing like deep affliction to smooth over hatred between two women; it was a pleasure to see them grieving and crying, leaning their heads together.

A few months later we all went our separate ways and that was the end of my father's house. When his house ends, that's when a man dies.

✕✕ S E V E N ✕✕
People Without Faces

I tried to maintain a cordial tone. Writing that first letter to Martha, after everything that had occurred between us, required a dual effort entailing caution on the one hand, boldness on the other. I told her about the sudden end to our expedition on the Mont des Enfants Perdus, including the theft of my field tent. I told the story in a rather cold, objective way, as if it had happened to someone else. I also told her about Thierry, and about his father who had been a hunter. I didn't mention what it was he hunted for.

Although I hadn't found a single trace of *Eleutherodactylus sanguineus*, I assured her that in a couple of weeks I'd try again on the same mountain, and in the meanwhile I'd stay in Port-au-Prince and use the time to locate the only Haitian who had become seriously interested in the declining populations, someone who wasn't even a herpetologist but a physician, a surgeon named Emile Boukaka.

I avoided talking about the city. I told her that the pool at the Oloffson was empty, that it was cleaned occasion-

ally. Two men in shorts would jump in and sweep up the
dry leaves, palm fronds, the half-rotten fruit, some scraps
of paper, and cram it all into plastic bags, then climb up
the ladder, drenched in perspiration that ran down their
backs as if they were really coming out of water. Then a
handful of guests would lie on lounge chairs and read the
French newspapers that arrived three or four days late.

And I didn't mention the dead bodies; I assumed
Martha knew about them from the papers. There was
always a small swarm of photographers on the streets of
Port-au-Prince, and every morning I saw them milling
around the bodies. The corpses, generally young men,
were discovered everywhere, but one morning the body of
a woman was found almost at the doors of the hotel. I
went over to look with the rest of the curious crowd. I
couldn't see her face, she was lying on her stomach, and
then I realized her hands were gone. I had no idea that the
corpse of a woman missing both hands could make so
strong an impression on me: I felt nauseated, and closed
my eyes.

My letter to Martha ended with several requests. In the
same envelope I included some papers and memos for my
colleagues; there was also a report for Vaughan Patterson,
written in longhand, and I asked her if she would have
time to type it.

My next move was to inform the embassy that I would
be in Haiti indefinitely, and to ask them if they could
include my correspondence in the diplomatic pouch. It
wasn't just any correspondence, after all, but documents,
notes, and photographs addressed to laboratories and uni-
versities.

That afternoon, as I was about to go out, a hotel

employee stopped me in the lobby: Some people were waiting to see me, he said, and pointed at two men in uniform who had stationed themselves in different locations; when they saw me they began to move in my direction. They identified themselves as police and asked for my passport. They stank of sweat. One of them had a broken nose, his upper lip had also been cut and the swelling reached all the way to his right cheek, and his right eye was swollen too; he was the one who did the talking. He wanted to know how long I planned to stay in Port-au-Prince.

My impulse was to be pleasant, and I asked them to sit down, but they shook their heads and remained standing, waiting.

"I'm a biologist," I said finally, "and I'm looking for a certain frog, not here, but on the Mont des Enfants Perdus."

I took a small sheet of paper from my pocket: It was the little frog I had sketched for Thierry at our first meeting. I didn't even use the scientific name, I called it the *grenouille du sang*, there it was, that was the only thing I was interested in.

"I have a permit from the Foreign Office," I added.

One passed the drawing to the other, and I realized they were scarcely looking at it. Still, they soiled the edges; I could see dirty fingerprints on the onionskin, black, perfect fingerprints. "Those permits aren't valid anymore," the one with the broken nose said abruptly. "All permits were canceled in September."

The other one handed back the drawing.

"You can't stay more than thirty days."

They bit off their words when they spoke, and it

occurred to me they might be impostors. I was about to ask them to show me their papers again—I had only seen a couple of wrinkled, damp-looking cards, I hadn't even checked the photographs. I stopped myself just in time, but I suppose my attitude must have changed.

"I plan to stay about three months," I said.

"No more than thirty days," the man repeated, and he handed me a paper as dirty as the edges of my picture: It was a subpoena.

"Bring your passport," he added, "and that permit from the Foreign Office."

I read the paper and folded it with the drawing, turned, and walked slowly toward the door; the two men stayed where they were, watching me move away, I walked faster and went out onto the smoke-filled streets. For a variety of reasons there was always dense smoke on the streets of Port-au-Prince; if they weren't burning piles of trash, they burned old furniture or tires, sometimes the bodies of dead animals were set on fire. That afternoon it was a burro, and I had the strange impression that the animal was moving its legs while it burned. I stopped to watch, a boy standing beside me laughed, a woman passed and shouted a few words at him I couldn't understand, they were harsh words, then the legs stopped moving and I continued on my way.

At the embassy I had to fill out a form that asked for my personal data, the reason for my presence in Haiti, and the person to be notified in case of sickness or death. I hesitated before writing down Martha's name, and beneath it I added my father's. The official who took care of me asked if I had a definite itinerary and I told him no, that my work depended on a series of expeditions, and they depended in turn on other factors such as rain, clouds, fog, even the phases of the moon. When the moon was full, anurans were much less active and possibly went into hiding, which was the reason so many expeditions failed.

The man listened attentively but refused to accept my correspondence, he first had to find out if it could be sent by pouch. In any event, he would have to fill out some other papers and suggested I call the next day when he could give me a definitive answer. I left the embassy, and when I was on the street I checked in my wallet for the address of the Haitian professor who had recommended Thierry; I wanted to ask him for the name of another guide. I thought I would tell him what had happened; some people just don't have the right chemistry and Thierry and I hadn't taken to each other. It would be difficult for me to work with him again after what had occurred on the first expedition.

I asked a passerby how to get to the address on the card. He told me it was some distance away, and I thought the best thing was to go back to the hotel and drive there in my car, the same Renault I had used to travel to the Mont des Enfants Perdus. One of the hotel employees who washed it had advised me to fill the tank; you never knew when gasoline would be unavailable.

I walked a few blocks and was back in the middle of a cloud of smoke, this time I couldn't tell the source but guessed it was an animal again. I decided to take another street, and when I turned the corner I felt my arm being pulled. I thought it was a peddler, I tried to shake loose, and that's when I was hit the first time, near my eyes, almost at the temple; the second punch landed right in my stomach. I fell down, tried to get up, but then I was kicked in the side, so hard I was afraid I'd been stabbed.

Two men held me down, somebody put his boot on my shoulder, a black, unpolished boot. Out of the corner of my eye I saw his other boot, and I saw two more boots, I thought they would kick me again, then I felt the tug, my hand was still holding the envelope with my correspondence, a large, padded envelope addressed to Martha. I tried to hold onto it and discovered that my fingers still responded, I tried to call for help, they pulled harder, another kick, and I passed out.

I believe I came to right away, because I was still sprawled in the middle of the sidewalk and people were standing around me. Then I thought of the corpses at dawn. Somebody helped me to my feet, but no one was brave enough to ask if I was all right or needed assistance. My left eye hurt and I could barely open it, my face burned, and I had trouble breathing. I walked the rest of the way to the hotel, holding myself up against the walls of buildings, but in the lobby I collapsed and two employees ran to help me. I asked them to take me to my room and call a doctor. A third person came up behind me and tried to support my head: It was Thierry.

That night he stayed with me. The ice packs the doctor prescribed for my eye had to be changed constantly, there was the possibility of a broken rib, and the slightest movement was painful, but even so I refused to go to a hospital. Every four hours I had to take two pills; Thierry placed them in the palm of my hand and I swallowed with difficulty, washing them down with some kind of warm infusion that he had prepared and brought in a thermos.

The pain grew worse in the middle of the night, I complained, and Thierry attempted to comfort me:

"Wait till dawn. Daybreak brings relief."

Neither of us really slept that night; I dozed off, sometimes I was delirious, I had no fever, but the sedatives gave me a feeling of unreality; it seemed to me that other people were walking in and out of the room, people without faces who came out of nothingness and dissolved back into nothingness.

Thierry was right: At first light my eye grew numb, the pain in my ribs eased, I fell into a deeper sleep and dreamed that my mother was trying to sketch the *grenouille du sang* and I was beside her, showing her the exact color she had to use.

The sound of voices woke me, and I could see with my good eye that a waiter was bringing in a breakfast tray. The doctor who had treated me the night before was also there, doing something to my left arm. He said good morning and asked if I was feeling better. I didn't answer right away, and he said my blood pressure was still very high.

"Perhaps it's due to the shock," he declared. "Do you want us to notify anyone?"

I shook my head, closed what was, for the moment, the one eye at my disposal—the other had been bandaged—and tried to remember the dream about my mother. I had the feeling that perhaps at this very moment, so many miles away, she was working on the only decent oil painting of her life: a little red frog looking out at the world from its bed of lilies. Speckled-brown lilies, that's what they had to be.

After breakfast I felt more energetic, I mentioned taking a shower, and the doctor recommended waiting until the next day, prescribed more pills, and then Thierry walked with him to the door. When he came back, he stopped to look out the window.

"They're still there," he said.

I realized I had lost the letter to Martha, the notes for my colleagues, and the report for Vaughan Patterson, a handwritten report documented with drawings and tapes recorded in the field.

Thierry closed the curtains and the room darkened.

"They want to be sure you understood the message," he remarked. "And don't tell me you don't know what message, because I gave it to you: The Mont des Enfants Perdus has its master, and he doesn't want you up there."

"I need that frog." My voice sounded different to me. "Tell them I'll get the frog and leave."

He sat at the foot of the bed.

"Every day you're more and more like Papa Crapaud. He went crazy over his animals too, looking for toads that never existed, that nobody knew about, not even my father or the oldest men. That's what he was like. I taught him the Law of Water."

I looked up at the ceiling and slid gently into the trap: I wasn't looking for an imaginary frog, I was looking for the *grenouille du sang*, the little red frog that he himself had heard so many times.

"So much the worse for me," sighed Thierry. "I'd be better off if I'd never heard it."

"That's beside the point," I told him. "What did Papa Crapaud die of?"

He shook his head and went back to the window, raised a corner of the curtain, stood there for some time.

"A woman killed him," he said without looking at me,

concentrating on the movement in the street. "I can teach you the Law of Water if you'll tell me about the birds your father raises."

I asked him to give me paper and pencil. When I began to draw, I became aware of how weak all my muscles were, and so the sketch I made of an ostrich turned out blurred, as if seen through a curtain of rain.

"This is the bird."

Beside it I drew a little man, small enough so that Thierry could estimate the size of the creature. He took the paper and looked at it in silence.

"How much meat can you get from the bird?"

"Enough to feed a hundred men," I answered.

"How many eggs does it lay?"

"That depends. On my father's farm one female laid ninety-five eggs in one year. But forty or fifty are enough."

"Enough for what?"

"To keep half the chicks," I said. "Then, after a year, you can take twenty-four or twenty-five birds to market. That's enough. You can sell the meat; there's a good market for the skin, and for the feathers."

He folded the paper, intending to keep it, and I promised him that later on I'd make him a better drawing.

"How many of these does your father have?"

I admitted that I didn't know exactly. The number changed every day, depending on the number of animals sold or slaughtered. I guessed he might own some sixty or seventy ostriches, not counting the chicks.

"How are they dangerous?"

He asked his questions and listened to my answers with the enlightened expression of a man hearing a powerful secret.

"Their claws are dangerous," I said. "Ostriches have two toes, only two, but they can decapitate a man, especially if it's rutting season and they're approached at dawn."

Thierry sighed, turned the drawing around, and asked me to tell him more: the color and size of the eggs, the time it took the chicks to hatch, what kind of food they ate. At that point I stopped, promised I'd tell him everything another time, but now I was exhausted and needed to sleep.

"Just one more thing," he pleaded. "Tell me how long they live."

Before going he left a good supply of ice where I could reach it, as well as the pills I was supposed to take in the afternoon. He walked out of the room, not making a sound, and I was reminded of Bengali servants in the movies, the ones who always end up stabbing their masters.

From the door he turned to look at me, and waved good-bye.

"It's not true that they bury their heads in the sand," I murmured, as if I were talking to myself. He was too far away to hear.

Every spring thousands of small, golden frogs belonging to the species known as *Bufo periglenes* would appear in the rivers and ponds of the Monteverde forest in northern Costa Rica.

It was the season when they engaged in a curious mating ritual that lasted for several days.

In 1988 only one golden frog was seen in the entire range of the forest.

Two years later, in 1990, the *Bufo periglenes* became completely extinct.

❌❖❌ EIGHT ❌❖❌

Cow Piss

He arrived loaded down with frogs. Black frogs like thunderstones. Pale frogs with the eyes of an owl. Yellow frogs the size of a coin.

He also had a toad never seen before, a rascally animal that was still moving inside its jar but looked more like a bat than a toad; I asked Papa Crapaud what kind of devil that was and he told me it was the most valuable one he had ever found. Then he started to draw it and showed me the paws, the flat head, the poison sacs, the flaps it used for leaping off the tops of trees. Papa Crapaud was very proud of the catch he had brought from Guadeloupe. But above all, he was proud of the woman he had found over there.

Her name was Ganesha. I was still young then and I had never seen another woman like her. Later on I saw lots of them with that same color, those same eyes, all of them wicked. Something in the combination doesn't go along with God. Papa Crapaud said that Ganesha's family, her mother and father, had come from very far away. He took out a map and showed me the four seas they'd had to cross to get to Guadeloupe. I asked him why they didn't just stay in their own country, but there was no need for him to answer: They didn't stay because it was written that they would have a daughter, it was written that on the day Papa Crapaud walked off the boat in the place called Pointe-à-Pitre, she would be the first to come up to him and try to sell him a dried frog. Later I found out she sold ornamental frogs at a kiosk in the port, that was how they saw each other for the first time.

The day he took me to meet her, Ganesha greeted me and clasped her hands together, her arms were very hairy and I bet to myself she had more than the three bushes my father liked so much. But she also wore a little ring in her nose and a blood mark on her forehead. I thought it was painted, nobody has a mark that red and round anywhere on their body.

She wasn't a very clean woman. My mother, who was, used to say that when a woman is a pig she always pulls the man down with her. I could prove that with Ganesha, because Papa Crapaud stopped wearing ironed shirts, and when he took out his handkerchiefs, they were white handkerchiefs, it was disgusting to see the dried snot, the sweat stains, a whole week's filth. Ganesha was so dirty she used cow piss to wash the floor, so dirty the neighbors complained because they couldn't stand the stink of cow dung coming out of her house.

Papa Crapaud was very offended when people complained about his woman, he raised his fist and shook it in the air, like he was defending his mother's honor. He even said that Ganesha wasn't like other women, and the *loas* that came down to her table were the *loas* of other lands

who liked cow piss and cow dung, cow dung and rice
milk. Nobody believed him, we all knew that Ganesha
had swallowed his soul. Papa Crapaud suffered that grief,
at first he hardly talked, you noticed it when it grew dark
and we were alone on the mountain; I would give him the
frogs I had caught, any frog that might interest him, and
then he would look at me and say: "Tell me, Thierry,
where is a man's dignity?" He asked me because he knew I
would answer: "A man's dignity is in his balls. That's why
he loses it so often."

And Ganesha wasn't a faithful woman either. When
Papa Crapaud went with me to the ponds, the men began
circling her house. Some went in, she decided which one
to let in, the rest stayed outside, looking at the house with
their mouths open, drooling with desire. Sometimes Papa
Crapaud came home unexpectedly and would let out a
bellow, take the broom and swing it through the air, the
men would move away and the first chance they had
they'd be back again, just like dogs running away and
coming back behind a bitch in heat.

Little by little he stopped making field trips, he didn't
want to leave Ganesha alone anymore. He beat her a lot
but she never came to her senses, she fell in love with a
man younger than Papa Crapaud, even younger than she
was, a drinker who scared away the rest of her suitors—he
was the one who could do it—and stole everything he
could lay his hands on: cameras and pens, dollars and
shoes, cakes of soap and mirrors, anything that Papa
Crapaud hadn't locked away.

I was the one who looked for all the frogs. The old
man told me to while he stayed home keeping an eye on
his wife, pretending he was drawing frogs. Once he even

put barbed wire around the windows and spent the nights standing guard at his own door, armed with an old carbine he bought from a *macoute* in Petit Goâve. That's how far a man of his learning fell, deep into that well, talking to himself at night. A frog's guts can't enlighten a man. Frogs were his whole world, that's why they betrayed him.

I asked him why he didn't take Ganesha back where he found her, and then Papa Crapaud, who didn't drink a drop of liquor, looked at me with a drunkard's eyes: "Where is a man's dignity?" He grabbed his privates and shook them at me. "Here it is, Thierry, and here I have nothing, nothing."

Ganesha, sitting on the floor, didn't even bother to look at us. She squatted when she cooked, she fixed stews the color of brick and served them in flowered bowls, the same bowls she had brought with her from Guadeloupe. When you least expected it she would jump up and run out of the house, Papa Crapaud ran after her and shouted insults, shook her, grabbed her by the throat and dragged her back to his lair. That's how they lived, that's how everybody's life changed, including mine, because even I wanted to know what that witch had between her legs. I stayed in the house one day when Papa Crapaud went out to mail some letters and I came up behind Ganesha and put my arms around her. She twisted and tried to run away, I caught her at the door, raised her skirt, and saw everything I had to see: black, straight hairs as long as a beard, I'd swear she combed them, she could have braided them. I moved them aside like I was opening a curtain and she let me touch her, I lifted her blouse and saw the nipples on her tits, as red as the blood mark on her forehead, I passed my tongue over them to lick away the paint, I thought it was paint, I rubbed them with saliva but they stayed red, that was their natural color. Then I pushed her down to the floor and she got free, but instead of hitting me or running away she went down on all fours and offered her rump like a dog. You didn't have to ask Ganesha for anything, that's why so many men were after her. She knew what each man needed.

From then on, whenever Papa Crapaud asked me where a man's dignity was, I didn't answer. Instead I would lower my eyes and change the subject, I was missing something too, something I lost on the day I fucked Ganesha and on all the days after that, all the days when I couldn't think about anything but how to fuck her again.

Then I got sick. I told my father and he didn't think it was too important, he just sent me to Divoine Joseph so he could give me a cure. Divoine had me strip like a *pwazon rat* in his crew, he examined me in front and behind, squeezed my foreskin, spread my cheeks, and felt under my balls.

"You're in trouble, sonny."

He gave me one potion to take and another to smear between my legs.

"You're better off doing it at one-armed Tancréde's place. The girls there are clean."

Papa Crapaud became very sick too. I asked him to let Divoine Joseph cure him but he refused, he went to see a doctor in Port-au-Prince, a white doctor who meant no harm and gave him injections for a long time but never really cured him.

Early one morning when we were on our way back from the river, he asked me why I had fucked his Ganesha, he asked the question with no anger, and I didn't answer.

Then it occurred to me that the reason was the cow piss. I said her smell was the same piss smell that was all over the house.

"That excites men," I told him, "that's why they come around like dogs, we're all like that when the smell of one animal's desire is on another."

"Ganesha has her beliefs," he replied, "the customs of her father and mother; don't you follow the customs of your parents?"

Then I remembered the Law of Water, it was a difficult law, I had never told him about it, not even after spending so many nights with him near the river, hearing noises not of this world, plague-ridden voices, splashes and cries on the water. I asked him if he wanted me to instruct him, I thought this was a way to make up for the harm I had done him under his own roof when I fucked that whore of a woman who I was dying to fuck again.

Papa Crapaud invited me to his house, something he hadn't done in many days; he asked Ganesha to bring us some tea and then leave us alone. He lit his pipe, his only luxury that hadn't been stolen, gave me a forgiving look, and sat down to listen.

"Blessed be Agwé Taroyo," I began. "The water puts out the flame."

✖✧✖ NINE ✖✧✖

Barbara

He asked me to turn off the tape recorder. The law he was about to teach me could exist only in the mind and on the tongue of men.

What you love, he said, you must respect, and the principle of all love is memory. I could commit his words to memory, and he advised me to learn them, but repeating them without the authorization of the "mysteries" brought severe punishment. Since he hadn't been able to save Papa Crapaud's life, perhaps now, after so many years, he could save the life of another frog hunter.

"Yours," he murmured, "which amounts to the same thing."

He lit a cigar and poured himself a glass of rum. The room was dark, and Thierry spoke quietly but repeated each sentence several times, as if he were dictating, monotonously and proudly, as if emotion kept him from raising his voice. When he took a breath he would raise the glass of dark rum to his mouth; it seemed to me his lips crackled when the liquor touched them.

"The ponds near the sea are not being fed enough. That is the first thing you must know."

He spoke in a kind of stupor, or trance, he lowered his eyelids, only a line of white was visible.

"Since they are not fed, they are always hungry, and since they are hungry, they swallow up everything they can. A man must take precautions when he comes close to these great, lonely pools."

I saw him shiver, I asked if he was cold, I suggested we turn off the air conditioner. He did not respond, he began to rock back and forth, very slowly. I thought he was about to topple over.

"Go and gather your frogs, I am not telling you not to, but be careful of looking into the eye of water, of stopping to talk to the woman who spreads her clothes on the shore. The woman is black, but her children may be mulattoes. If they call to you, say nothing and hurry on, for they are not of this world. But if you see a mangy buzzard, speak to her immediately, say 'Kolé kolé yo la,' repeat it three times and cross yourself in the name of God."

I recalled that Martha would always cross herself before she got into bed. At first it seemed ironic that a woman of her character, with her scientific training, would have kept that childish habit, like someone who has kept an old teddy bear and hugs it when it's time to go to sleep. She would never tell me the origin of that mania, by this time it was only a silly mania, but I suppose it had to do with the notions of the old woman who raised her. Martha went to live with her grandparents before she was two, and from then on she saw her parents for only short periods, usually at Christmas, her mother was ill, a cyclical depressive. I didn't meet them until the day of our wedding, suddenly they showed up, like two phantoms, and I spent my time observing them: Martha looked like her mother, especially around the eyes, and she had the same way of pursing her mouth; she didn't resemble her father at all, except perhaps in the timbre of her voice.

"Do not lie down to sleep under any tree. You need special knowledge to tell which is clean and which is full."

Thierry's glass was empty, he groped for the bottle and filled it again; he threw his head back and it seemed to me his voice changed.

"If you see a crab near a house, call the owner, call for him in a loud voice, because that animal does not travel alone. Crabs have their work, they fill themselves with 'harm' and then go out so that someone will take it from them. There are very few left who know how to do this work, but just in case, you should yell at him that you don't want it."

Boiled crab. Crab cakes à la parmigiana. Eggs scrambled with creamed crab. Part of the menu at Crab Stories, Martha's favorite restaurant, a place where she would have lunch with Barbara at least twice a week. She asked me there one night and had me try some fried shellfish, a delicious dish that filled me with suspicions.

"Do not say the names of your loved ones while the water is around your waist; do not make plans or think of celebrations when your feet are in the water; do not even recall those who have passed, the dead spend time playing in the weeds, they suck at the living man from down below, they drown him without meaning to."

A few years later, Martha's mother died. They called us just before dawn; almost all sudden deaths seem to happen then. I went with my wife to the funeral and saw that the dead woman had her lips pursed, my mother-in-law had suffered a stupid death: She fell in her own house and her head split open like a fruit. Martha didn't shed a single tear, but she was devastated when her grandmother died a few months later. She wanted to have the wake in our house, she had just met Barbara, they had become friends on some ecological excursions and from then on saw each other practically every day. Barbara helped her organize the wake, she was courteous, she embraced me politely. Then she stationed herself beside my wife and stayed there until it was time for the burial: rubbing her back, bringing her food, going with her to the bathroom.

"Do not dare to eat papaya when the lagoon is in sight. Do not even think about cutting guanabanas or peeling mangoes if you think the scent may reach the water. Do not split a single coconut if it seems the sound may reach the shore. Do what I say."

After the burial we went back to the house. Barbara came with us, she took charge in the kitchen and prepared supper; she was a very practical woman, the kind of person who inspires certainties, probably the very ones she is lacking. In the middle of supper she offered my wife a glass of wine, and my wife kissed her on the cheek in gratitude.

"If a man kisses a woman's feet in the water, the woman will die before him."

Thierry stood, gestured languidly, then made another brief, too brief, gesture of joy. I had the impression he was waking after sleeping for many hours. Then he wiped his eyes, it seemed he was wiping away tears, but there were no tears, only their memory.

"If two women step with the same foot, at the same time, into the mouth of the river where the fresh and salt waters meet, they will love each other like man and woman."

"Like man and woman." I shuddered. Which of them was the man? Or did they perhaps love each other like woman and woman? Who seduced whom, which of them took the initiative, what did they say about me (something is always said), what did Martha allege about me, what memories, reproaches, frustrations did she confess?

"Do not drink the water of a pond without asking permission and without paying the price."

What Martha had seen in me, with her trained marine biologist's eyes, she talked about with Barbara, their arms around one another, in that apartment I didn't know but suspected was filled with photographs—a successful geologist always has her picture taken in situ—studded with stones and fossils, soil samples and rock fragments that had fallen as far as they could go.

"To take a stone from a pond, you will have to kneel and ask if you can. You never took one out, did you?"

I gestured to Thierry to be quiet and closed my eyes. I suddenly felt desperate and tried to concentrate on my recovery—every blow I had received still hurt—and on the approximate date when we could set out for Casetaches. That was the only thing I should care about. I opened my eyes; they had been burning, now they were on fire.

"My wife left me, Thierry. I don't want to talk about water. When do you think we'll be able to climb the mountain?"

"Casetaches? Whenever you want, whenever you feel better. This week."

"This week," I decided. "But now tell me, how did Papa Crapaud die?"

In 1992, David Whistler, curator of the Museum of Natural History in Los Angeles, investigated the populations of the toad *Bufo marinus* in the Hawaiian archipelago.

On the island of Kauai, where the species had once been plentiful, he could not find a single specimen of the animal, alive or dead.

The natives reported that the toads simply had "gone away."

XOX TEN XOX

You, Darkness

On the banks of the Bras à Gauche, which is the gentlest river I know, you can smell the stink that rises from the Bras à Droit, which is the dirtiest. These two rivers join in a whitewater called Saut du Clerc, and from there they flow as one, not as gentle and not as dirty, a single green, rough current that opens into the sea near Jérémie.

The "mysteries" have their whims, and instead of going to eat at the Bras à Gauche, which always smells wonderful, they insist on accepting their due in the Bras à Droit, which stinks to high heaven. Papa Crapaud didn't want to believe it, and one night I took him to see for himself: With his own eyes he saw an old woman named Passionise going into the river, carrying in one hand the tray with live chickens, food, syrup, and in the other, wrapped in newspaper, fine sweets from Dominica. The old woman sank with all that abundance, she stayed under water a long time, she must have been setting the table for Agwé Taroyo, and she didn't drown. When they played the drum she came back, very satisfied. One of her sons always stayed on shore, this son brought his drum and when he decided his mother was ready to leave the bottom, he beat the drum good and hard and the drumbeats helped her find the way back.

Papa Crapaud was very fond of the two rivers, especially the Bras à Gauche, where he found his toad. There was a time, before he came back with Ganesha, when we would set up camp on the banks. He would go to sleep after breakfast and wake up when it was getting dark, which was when the animal woke up too. Then he spent the nights looking at it, taking notes on the sounds it made, keeping track of how many times it mated—and it was a lot, that was the horniest damn toad I ever saw—counting the eggs the female laid and putting a tadpole under the magnifying glass while it was still alive. Papa Crapaud gave it his own name, a name that was too long for such a troublesome toad, light purple with a flat head and little white spots around the eyes. Years later the animal disappeared, it just left, vanished like so many others.

It was a happy time for Papa Crapaud. They sent him an illustration, a sketch in color of the toad, with his name underneath in big letters. It was an illustration from a book, and he put it in a frame and hung it in his house. Maybe that was why—because he had been so lucky on that river—that was why, when he couldn't watch Ganesha anymore, he said he wanted to go back to the Bras à Gauche with me, he said he wanted to record the haunts of the black-lipped frogs, he bought a van to take him across the countryside and we set up camp near the Saut du Clerc. We spent three days there not doing anything, the poor old man just shook whenever he went near the water, but he didn't want to go back to Jérémie.

I thought he had the sickness again in his privates, and I offered to take him to Divoine Joseph, he grumbled and said it wasn't necessary. We just stayed there, looking at each other, and that night, when I brought him his soup, he grabbed my arm and confessed that he'd been poisoned. I asked him who had given him the poison and he didn't say anything: That meant the guilty one was Ganesha, and I said that as soon as the sun came up, whether he wanted me to or not, I'd go find Divoine Joseph so he could purge him. Besides curing bad diseases, Divoine knew the remedy for almost every poison.

Papa Crapaud groaned louder and louder, he said it felt like all the ants in the world were crawling around under his skin. He couldn't sleep and we talked till dawn, he wanted to know what kind of poison it was, he didn't come right out and say so but I could tell because of the questions he asked me. I explained that poison was prepared one way in Saint Marc and another way in Gonaïves, but since Ganesha's lover was from the village of Léogane, I was sure they had given him one from around there. Just one, because they made two poisons in Léogane, each from a different animal. I had a lump in my throat when I told him that feeling ants under his skin was a sign he'd taken the one made from toads. It wasn't fair, it wasn't right that he should die of poison from the *crapaud blanc*, it may have been mixed with poison from the *crapaud brun*.

"It is fair," said Papa Crapaud. "It's only right that toads take me from this world."

He tried to smile but his mouth twisted, then he asked if any fish gave poison. I told him there were two: one they call *bilan* and the other *crapaud de mer*; both swelled up if you just touched them with the end of a stick, and gave off a bitter poison. He asked me where I had learned so much about poisons and I told him that Charlemagne Compère, Yoyotte Placide's foster brother, prepared them in Gonaïves. A couple of times I had seen Charlemagne preparing the little packets of powder, and to do it he smeared his hands with *clairin*, ammonia, and lemon juice, plugged up his nostrils, covered his whole body with jute sacks, and put a hat on top of that. The men who made poison were careful not to touch it or breathe it in, and even so, sometimes they died.

Papa Crapaud went on asking questions but I closed my mouth. I remembered that in Gonaïves, to make the powder stronger, they would put a toad and a snake together in a jar; the jar was buried and left long enough for the creatures to die of rage. Then they took out the dead animals, dried them and ground them up, and added them to the mixture. It didn't seem Christian to tell him about it that night, not while Papa Crapaud was so sick, and I pretended I was too tired and he said the ants in his body were easing up and that we should go to sleep.

I was glad to hear it, and I curled up in my bag, I dreamed about my mother and my dead friends, but above all I dreamed about the crazy woman I had once brought down from Casetaches Hill. In my dream I couldn't see her but I knew she was there because I heard her words, words from her mouth, much longer and much more difficult than those from her heart. This was when the call of an owl woke me, at first I thought it was an owl but suddenly I realized it was Papa Crapaud. I took the flashlight and sat down beside him: A little trickle of blood came out of his nose, he wasn't moving or breathing, and another little trickle came out of his mouth. I remembered a phrase my father would say when he greeted a dead man, something they always said in Guinea: "The soul of the fallen flies away, free, from the tip of the arrow called Erikuá."

I prayed for him, I took off his shirt and wiped away the blood that was beginning to dry. I put the shirt in my knapsack because it was filled with the virtue of death. I dressed him in another shirt that wasn't as dirty—I told you before that Papa Crapaud became careless about his clothes after he started living with Ganesha; then I put the body in the van and drove it to his house. I didn't knock at the door, first I looked in the window and saw that Ganesha was on her knees surrounded by smoke and damp dung, surrounded by that smell of cow piss, praying to the virgin with all those arms, the one she called Mariamman. She repeated the prayer several times: "O toi, lumière . . . Toi, l'Immaculée, toi, l'obscurité qui enveloppe l'esprit de ceux qui ignorent ta gloire."

I imagined she was praying for the soul of Papa Crapaud, since she must have known he was dead; of all the women I've known in my life, Ganesha was the most corrupt. I walked around and knocked on the door, she took a while to open it, and when she finally did I saw that she had been sweating, her orange-colored tunic stuck to her skin because of the sweat, and big drops ran down her cheeks and chest.

"I brought him home."

She covered her head with a white shawl she had draped around her shoulders.

"The family is going to want all his papers," I told her. "God help you if you touch them."

The two of us took the body from the van and laid it on the bed. I told Ganesha I was going to bring a doctor to find out what had killed him.

"This killed him," she said, touching her red tit through the wet cloth.

Papa Crapaud's wife and his children, who were grown men and had their own families, lived too far away to come in time. So it was up to us, to Ganesha and me, to watch over him that night and say good-bye to him the next day. A friend of his came from Port-au-Prince, and with me and Ganesha watching he packed boxes with the preserved frogs, and Papa Crapaud's papers and drawings. He gave away his clothes to everybody there, he offered me a pair of shoes but I never keep the shoes of the dead, it's bad to look at them, imagine wearing them.

Even Ganesha's lover, the man from Léogane, received his gift. They gave him a pair of pants and a tee-shirt that was almost new, and he was glad to take them, even though he asked if he could have the shoes I had turned down. He said it very humbly, as if he hadn't already stolen enough.

The doctor came and said just what Ganesha had said: Papa Crapaud's heart had broken, it probably had been sick for many years. That's something else about the powders, they're invisible to science, the little bit of science that doctors have, I mean. Divoine Joseph, who knew so much and was enlightened, would have known which powder it was just by smelling the dead man's head.

At dawn we went out to bury him. The priest from the church in Jérémie came with us, and a professor from Cap-Haïtien who arrived at the last minute, he was a fine mulatto who wiped away his tears. Ganesha began to burn incense and gave each of us a paper cone of flower petals to toss onto the casket. My brother Jean Pierre came with me, and Carmelite, Frou-Frou's daughter, she was there too, dressed in black and wearing the straw hat that belonged to her mama. She looked good and I asked her to take a walk after the burial, but she said she wouldn't do it on the mountain anymore, that when Jean Pierre or I wanted to lie with her we'd have to take her to our own bed and let her stay. That's what her mother had told her.

I thought about it and decided it didn't suit me. Bringing her to my bed was like telling everybody, Frou-Frou and my brothers and sisters—my father had died a few months before—that I took her as my wife and the mother of my children. And I didn't love her that much. Besides, I had plans to move to Port-au-Prince; now that my father and my second father, Papa Crapaud, were dead, there was nothing to hold me in Jérémie. Or maybe one thing held me, something I didn't understand then, it was my heart's secret.

At the same time, under that same sun in the cemetery, I think my brother Jean Pierre also began to want to put his arms around Carmelite, and she told him the same thing she had told me. But my brother was very weak, or maybe the smell of the dead confused him, I don't know, he swallowed the bait and the next day the girl woke up in his bed, the whole family celebrated and Frou-Frou took me aside and warned me that from now on I couldn't touch my sister-in-law. Now Carmelite was my sister-in-law. Paul couldn't lay a finger on her either. The youngest of my mother's brood, a wild boy, he would always pinch her rump and hug her in front of everybody, Carmelite would struggle to get free and he would hold her even tighter and kiss her on the mouth. It was like a game, a dangerous game, because Paul was the only one who couldn't accept losing her. First he had a big fight with her, one afternoon he started to beat her and Frou-Frou interfered, Jean Pierre interfered, we all did some shouting that day. Carmelite cried and Paul swore by our dead mother that he would leave the house, but he never did.

So you see, that all began at the burial of Papa Crapaud, and other things too that you wouldn't believe. When we finished throwing the petals on the casket, Ganesha asked me to come live with her and I felt like spitting in her face. I looked at the man from Léogane, he was watching us from a distance, he was trying to guess what we were saying.

"I don't want anybody to steal from me," I said.

She threw herself at my feet, she began to cry and wail.

"Go back to Guadeloupe. Go there and live with all your filth."

Papa Crapaud was dead and buried. Death always wins if God doesn't oppose it. Each of us went our separate ways, and I left with a clear conscience: I had sewn the lips of the dead man and put a knife in his hands, I did it fast so the priest from Jérémie wouldn't know. Papa Crapaud's corpse was safe: The man from Léogane and his pals couldn't wake him; they couldn't steal his bones, or pull out his teeth, or tear off the piece of skin around his privates.

The next day I went to the grave and found the earth dug up. I felt satisfied when I saw that my suspicions were right, a man always proves himself on the ashes of another, and I proved myself with Papa Crapaud. I took a handful of that dirt and kissed it, spread it on my face, rubbed it on my head. Some of the earth fell into my eyes, went into my mouth. Some of it went down my throat and then I was at peace inside.

At peace means with grief in its proper place.

❌❖❌ E L E V E N ❌❖❌
Indian Hut

We didn't go to Jérémie that week or the next week either. We left twenty days later, on a Tuesday, after I'd seen the doctor recommended by the embassy. He was an elderly Haitian, very short and somewhat brusque, who spent a long time palpating my bones and examining me with a stethoscope. He also drew blood samples, and with the results in hand he came to tell me I was cured.

My recuperation took longer than expected because of an enlarged vein, a kind of dark-green tumor at the height of my knee, a hard, painful ball that would not go down for days. I used the time to research the species mentioned by Thierry. *Osteopilus dominicencis* was the scientific name for a variety of toad that was fairly common on Hispaniola. It could be white, and then it was called *crapaud blanc*, or brown, and then the name changed to *crapaud brun*. What was known in Haiti as the *bilan* was simply the *Diodon hola-canthus*, a spine-covered fish also called the guanabana fish. As for the *crapaud de mer*, I learned it was the *Sphoeroides tes-tudineus*, the most poisonous species in these waters.

One afternoon a man came to see me in the company of the hotel manager: He said he was from the police and wanted details of the assault; he asked if I suspected anyone or wanted to file a complaint. I thought it prudent to say I could hardly remember a thing, and suspected no one. I added that all I wanted was to recover so I could travel to Jérémie, and somehow I let him know that I wouldn't go back to the Mont des Enfants Perdus.

He seemed satisfied, and promised that the investigation would continue and they'd keep me informed; the manager only bowed his head, he was a distinguished-looking mulatto with a quiet voice who did not wish to intervene more than absolutely necessary. When they left I decided to call Martha. I had been waiting for the right moment, it was New Year's Eve, a date that intimidates me and that I loathe with all my heart, which is why I felt like placing the call. It took them more than a quarter of an hour to connect me, and when I finally heard her voice, something very strange happened, I became disoriented for a second and asked who I was talking to; very discreetly she said, "It's me," she recognized my voice right away and was self-assured enough to wait and say nothing. "It's Victor," I said in a strangled voice. She didn't speak right away, first she cleared her throat: "You vanish like a ghost and now suddenly you reappear."

I told her about the theft of the letters and the report for Vaughan Patterson, but as I spoke I noticed that my words sounded false, as if I were inventing an excuse, a wild story, something even I had trouble believing. I didn't mention the beating; I would have liked to cause her concern but the entire incident was rather humiliating and I wasn't sure what effect it would have on her.

For a long time Martha didn't say a word, she was listening to me, I suppose, and then she interrupted: "Listen, I have something to tell you." It was my turn to be silent, and I felt the vein in my knee begin to throb; I moved my leg and the throbbing stopped. "I wrote you a letter," she continued, "and I want to know where to send it." I waited a few seconds, I thought about asking her just to tell me what it was, to do it on the phone, a single blow, rapid and precise. Instead I said I was staying at the Oloffson Hotel but in a few days I'd be leaving for Jérémie, and the best thing was to write to me in care of the embassy; I gave her the address and she repeated it to make sure she had it right. Then she gave me some messages left by my colleagues; Patterson had called too, trying to locate me, but Martha couldn't help him very much: "I told him I didn't know anything about you." At this point the conversation languished and ended as abruptly as it had begun, with no good wishes for the new year; neither one of us wanted to mention it, that would have been too much. When I hung up I was filled with a kind of shame, or mute rage; I regretted not asking what I clearly was obliged to ask. In situations like this a man has to know certain details. I picked up the receiver to call her again but hung up immediately. In situations like this a man needs all his self-control.

By the time I could finally walk again, Thierry had located Dr. Emile Boukaka, a surgeon and an amateur herpetologist. Months earlier I had read one of his articles in *Froglog* on the decline of amphibians; it was a brief piece but I made a file for it and decided to write to him. I never imagined at the time that I would meet him face-to-face in Port-au-Prince. He sent me his card through

Thierry, fine gray stock with gray-blue lettering; I called and we made an appointment.

The day before we were to leave for Jérémie, I went to number 77 rue Victor Severe, a brick house that had no shingle. Only at the top of the stairs, a few steps made of shoddy cement, rough cement that scraped at the soles of my shoes, did I see a nameplate: EMILE BOUKAKA, CABINET. I rang the bell and a neatly dressed girl opened the door, led me straight to her small desk, and we both remained standing while she looked for my name in an old appointment book. Then she asked me to have a seat. At that hour there were no patients, and since there were no magazines or newspapers either, I concentrated on a large poster, stained with mildew, that hung directly in front of me:

> Toad, that under cold stone
> Days and nights hast thirty-one
> Swelter'd venom sleeping got,
> Boil thou first i' the charmed pot.

Next to the poster was a kind of bulletin board with a number of postcards pinned to the cork. I went over to look at them, they were from all over the world, France for the most part, but also some unexpected places, Bombay, for example, Nagasaki, Buenos Aires, even Bafatá. The girl had left the room, and out of curiosity I took down some cards: most were simply greetings and regards, or data related to the disappearance of some amphibian. One, however, attracted my attention more than the others: Under a shelter three naked Indian women were squatting down and cooking, and behind them a very old man, who was naked as well, stared belligerently into the camera. The card seemed very old, and it was hand-painted; in one corner, in tiny letters, was the caption: INDIAN HUT, BENI, BOLIVIA.

On the other side were a few lines written in a mix of English and French:

"*De Pérou, une photo de mes cher anthropophages. Kisses to Duval, is he still in Port-au-Prince?*"

It was signed at the bottom with the initials C.Y.

I looked for a date but didn't see one, I replaced it, and at that moment was startled by a honeyed-almond voice, almost a woman's voice:

"*Et bien*, where are the blessed frogs going?"

I had thought that Emile Boukaka was a mulatto; nobody had told me so but I had an image of him as a tall, gray-haired light-skinned man with spectacles, more self-conscious, less chubby and tropical than he actually was. Boukaka wore a green shirt with hibiscus flowers on it, and he was absolutely black, intensely black, the skin on his arms gleamed as if he had been born in Africa. His hair and beard were somewhat reddish, and he had an enormous round, flat face, a face like a Mexican (or Bolivian?) tortilla patted into shape by naked Indian women. There, in the fat circle of that face, his nose, his bulging eyes, his thick half-smiling lips seemed to be dancing.

"They're all going to leave us," he added. "I know you're looking for the *grenouille du sang*."

I smiled, and Boukaka gestured for me to follow him. He led me down a hallway filled with night photographs; I recognized some species, most were from the Amazon. Then we came to an office painted yellow; more photos were hanging there, and I stopped in front of an imposing, gigantic, purple image: It was the *Eleutherodactylus san-guineus.*

"They're leaving or they're hiding," he insisted. "Or they're simply letting themselves die. Nothing is clear, nobody wants to talk about it."

"I do," I said. "I came to talk to you."

He showed me a copy of a report he had been working on for several years. He took out more photographs, opened a cabinet and showed me fifteen or twenty preserved frogs. The *grenouille du sang* was not among them, though he said he had often seen it when he was a boy, and later, in his youth, he had caught one. His father, who had also been a physician and a student of batrachians, used to take him along on his expeditions to the Mont des Enfants Perdus. But those had been different times, before the place had been turned into the hell it later became.

"Nowadays no one would even think about going on that mountain," he added.

"I did," I replied, with some irony, "and so did the guide who works with me. His name is Thierry Adrien and he worked with Jasper Wilbur more than thirty years ago."

"That Thierry . . ." Boukaka murmured, not finishing the sentence. "I didn't know Wilbur, but he was a good friend of my father's. He died suddenly, and my father was the one who went to Jérémie to collect his things."

I was about to ask if he knew the circumstances of Jasper Wilbur's death, but decided I shouldn't distract him or change the subject. Then I spoke to him about Casetaches Hill, we discussed for some time the possibility of finding *Eleutherodactylus sanguineus* there, not more than a handful of individuals but I'd settle for a single

frog so I could keep my promise to Vaughan Patterson.
Boukaka shook his head and I attempted to persuade him.
They'd said, for example, that the Wyoming toad had disappeared. Dr. Baxter, who discovered it, was the first to
raise the alarm, and then in 1983 his assistants admitted
there was nothing else to do, nowhere else to look. I had
put it in my file of extinct species. And had kept it there
until 1987, when a fisherman saw it in a pond south of
Laramie. True, it was just one colony with fewer than a
hundred members. But it was the *Bufo hemiophrys*, no doubt
about it, Baxter's favorite animal. They say the man wept
when he saw it again.

"Do you know what the farmers say on Gonâve
Island?"

Boukaka circled the room and stopped right behind
me; it was difficult for me to hear and accept that voice, a
thin, musical thread, and not be able to look into his face.

"They say that Agwé Taroyo, the god of waters, has
called the frogs down to the bottom. They say they have
seen them leave: Freshwater animals diving into the sea,
and the ones that don't have the time or strength to reach
the meeting place are digging holes in the ground to hide,
or letting themselves die along the way."

Boukaka came back into view, holding a pipe in his
mouth; the pipe was cold, and he sat down again at his
desk and began to fill it with tobacco.

"It seems absurd, doesn't it? . . . Well, some fishermen
from Corail who were casting their nets near Petite
Cayemite reported pulling hundreds of dead frogs from
the water, and when they came to the beach, a little rocky
beach on the island, they found the birds devouring thousands of other frogs. That was two weeks ago."

The aroma was very strong, cinnamon mixed with something else I couldn't identify: perhaps anise or mint; I had a hunch it might have been eucalyptus.

"Do you know what a voodoo song says, a song they sing to greet Damballah Wedó?"

I shook my head, I thought Boukaka's almond voice was a singer's voice. It didn't go with his face, or his bus driver's belly, or the sparse hairs of his beard, a meager beard that surely had stopped growing.

"Damballah is a silent deity, the only mute god in the pantheon. The song goes like this: 'Toad, give your voice to the serpent, the frogs will show you the way to the moon, when Damballah desires it, the great flight will begin.'"

Boukaka lowered his head, he seemed exhausted; the smell of his pipe began to make me feel tired too.

"The great flight has begun," he repeated. "You people invent excuses: acid rain, herbicides, deforestation. But the frogs are disappearing from places where none of that has happened."

I wondered who he meant by "you people." You people, the professional herpetologists. Or you people, the biologists who hold their conferences in Canterbury, in Nashville, in Brasilia, hold them behind closed doors and walk out more perplexed than when they came in. You people, fearful, finicky people, incapable of looking at the dark, recalcitrant, atemporal side of the decline.

"I have no excuses," I said. "Nobody knows what's going on."

We spent more time talking about other species; I made an effort to handle with some grace the enormous quantity of data provided by Boukaka. I was amazed by his capacity for detail, his precision, I can even say his erudition. When we said good-bye he shook my hand; I was about to tell him that he reminded me of a famous musician, I had been trying to think who it was he resembled and then I looked into his eyes and decided it was Thelonious Monk. It may have been irrelevant but I remembered a composition of Monk's that wasn't played too often: "See You Later, Beautiful Frog."

"What I've learned, I learned in books," Boukaka said emphatically from the door. "But what I know, everything I know, I took from fire and water, from water and flame: One puts out the other."

On that overcast Tuesday in the middle of January when we finally set out for Jérémie, I still had not received Martha's letter, but I had no doubt what it would say.

Thierry was driving, telling me a love story, his fingers clutching at the steering wheel, his eyes fixed on the road, not much more than a rutted trail. He spoke in a very sweet voice, he didn't even look as old. Suddenly he said something that struck me: A man never knows when the grief begins that will last forever. I looked at him and saw a tear running down his cheek.

"Not grief, not joy," I said very quietly. "A man never knows anything, Thierry, that's his affliction."

Studies carried out since August 1989 indicate that three species of frog of the type *Eleutherodactylus*, commonly called *coquí*, have disappeared from the rain forests of Puerto Rico.

Eleutherodactylus jasperi (the golden *coquí*), *Eleutherodactylus karlschmidt* (the palmate *coquí*), and *Eleutherodactylus eneidae* (the Eneida *coquí*) are considered extinct.

Eleutherodactylus locustus (the little hammer *coquí*) and *Eleutherodactylus richmondi* (the Richmond *coquí*) are on the verge of extinction.

❊❊❊ T W E L V E ❊❊❊
Julien

My heart's secret was revealed on the night I told them I was moving to Port-au-Prince.

I could see that my brother Jean Pierre was very sad; he said if it wasn't for Carmelite and the child on the way, he would come with me. My brother Paul had been crazed for months, it seemed to me he hardly even cared that I was going. He wasn't fighting anymore with Carmelite, he didn't even look at her, her belly was beginning to show and he swallowed his bile. The pregnant belly of someone else's woman is always like a part of the other man.

By the time he was thirteen or fourteen, Julien, the boy my father had with Frou-Frou, stopped playing *macoute perdu* and joined the flesh-and-blood *macoutes*, he became one of them. Since he looked older than he really was, he lied to get into the army. He would come home after midnight and get up at dawn; he didn't talk much with his mother, he talked only a little to Carmelite, his half sister, he hardly talked at all to his half brother Jean Pierre. That must have been why he was like a stranger, a half brother to everyone and a half son to his own mother because my mother was the one who raised him.

Frou-Frou wanted to know when I planned to leave and I said in three or four days. She offered to wash my clothes and asked in an offhand way if Papa Crapaud's wife was going with me too. Jean Pierre poked me with his elbow, Carmelite started to laugh, and Paul looked at me in confusion, expecting who knows what answer.

"I don't go with my friends' women," I said. "Least of all that one, she's an evil snake."

It seems Frou-Frou didn't really believe me. My father had told her about the sickness Divoine Joseph had cured, everybody knew it came from Ganesha. Jean Pierre poked me again and said in Port-au-Prince I'd get tired of fucking, what they had there was plenty of women. Frou-Frou reminded him that we were eating and to save his filth for the street, then she offered again to wash my clothes, and I remembered the knapsack she packed for me the night my father sent me to find the woman on Casetaches. When I came back from that mountain she had washed my clothes too, and cleaned my shoes all stained with blood, and mended my shirt, she washed it first and then she mended it, it was stiff with bitter sweat, the sweat of fear. I looked at Frou-Frou and for the first time saw what she always had been: a good woman.

That night Julien came home earlier than usual and said they were sending him to Gonaïves the next day and he had to pack his things. Nobody dared to ask who was sending him so far away or what he would do there. Julien was the youngest in the family, but he seemed to rule over all of us; he reminded me so much of my father when he came home from his hunts, you never wanted to say anything to him. I found out later that even Frou-Frou, though she was his mother, didn't really trust him, she never knew him inside and that always makes you afraid.

When the house was quiet and everybody was in bed, I took my dirty clothes to Frou-Frou's room. She was packing a knapsack for Julien and I stayed, watching her fold two or three changes of clothes. She brought no love to the work, you could see it in her movements, she was very tired or maybe very sad; suddenly she raised her head and called to Julien, asking where his handkerchiefs were. Julien shared a room with Paul right next to hers, there was a thin partition, my father put up the partition when Frou-Frou came to live in our house.

He must have been asleep because he didn't answer. Frou-Frou shrugged, then closed the knapsack and put it on the floor. I was behind her, holding all my clothes in my arms, and when I saw her bend down I remembered something else, I remembered the times I'd seen her dancing at the banquets that Yoyotte Placide arranged. The last time she danced her blouse had slipped off and all the women came to cover her and she dropped to the floor and her belly began to jump around as if she had a little animal inside. Jean Pierre and I, we must have been around nine years old then, spent a lot of time talking about Frou-Frou's breasts, about how they had popped out. Then I forgot about them until that night, when it all came back to me. She took the dirty clothes from my arms and tossed them on the bed; the clothes were scattered all over the bed and she began to separate the colors, she separated the colored shirts from the white ones. Her back was to me again, she probably thought I had gone but I went up to her, I didn't make any noise, and then she had to know I had stayed because I pressed up against her and she didn't move, I put my arms around her tight, as if I wanted to break her in half, and kissed her on the neck. Frou-Frou asked me to leave her be, she said it very quietly so Julien and Paul wouldn't hear; very quietly, so I wouldn't really leave her be. I felt her letting go, I turned her around and kissed her on the mouth, I pushed her onto the bed and whispered that I remembered her breasts, she sat up and opened her blouse, she leaned over my body and took her breasts in her hands and showed them to me. They were the same as the breasts at the banquet, the same ones uncovered in the dance when her cousins ran to cover them again, the ones that provoked my mother to fury and left Yoyotte Placide with a grief-stricken face.

That was my heart's great secret, I knew it as soon as Frou-Frou took away her hands and I put mine there; I sighed so loud she told me to be quiet, you could hear everything in that house: my father's sighs when he made love to my mother; my father's sighs when he made love to Frou-Frou; and recently Jean Pierre's sighs when he made love to Carmelite—Paul heard them too, those sighs tormented him more than any other.

You never heard anything from the women. Not even that night, not even from Frou-Frou who had been so long without a man. She closed her mouth and didn't open it except to kiss me or let herself be kissed.

We finished very late and Frou-Frou didn't ask me again to leave her be. She slept a little and I stayed at her side, thinking how strange the world was, thinking about what my father would have thought if he could see me there in his bed, enjoying the mother of his child, the last of his brood.

When it was almost dawn, but still dark, I woke Frou-Frou. She muttered something and opened her arms. For a man there's nothing in this world like fucking a woman who's asleep. Or half asleep. I don't know what she was dreaming about, but this time she was the one who sighed so loud I covered her mouth. I covered it and uncovered it, and one of those times she bit my hand, she bit it in her sleep and sighed even louder, I think she shouted. I thought about praying that nobody heard us, but you can't pray when you're naked, especially not when you're inside a woman.

Then we were quiet. When I couldn't sleep anymore and wanted to get up, Julien came in. He had come for his knapsack and he stopped in front of the bed, he was carrying a flashlight and he shined that flashlight on my face, on the two of us, and our eyes met. He looked just like my father, he smelled the same, he had the same mouth, that mouth he hardly ever opened to talk. He didn't say a thing, he lowered the flashlight and picked up his pack; Frou-Frou was sound asleep and never knew that her son had seen us naked with our arms around each other, tangled in my dirty clothes, the colored shirts all mixed up with the white ones.

We pretended in front of Jean Pierre and Carmelite, in front of my brother Paul. One night, when we were sitting at the table, I said I would stay another two weeks and wait for a friend who also wanted to move to Port-au-Prince. Every night, when the house was dark, I hurried to Frou-Frou's bed, and if I was late she would complain or pretend to be asleep—she knew I liked to wake her.

This was when our brother Etienne came back to Jérémie; he was on his way to La Cahouane to look for wood for his father-in-law's carpentry shop. He ate with us, made jokes about Carmelite's belly, and tried to convince Paul to join him, he wanted Paul to go with him to La Cahouane and then back to Côteaux. He offered him a job in the carpentry shop and Paul said yes.

He asked me what work I would do in Port-au-Prince and I said whatever turned up, then he put his arm around my shoulder and said, as if he knew everything, that I shouldn't take Frou-Frou there until I had a good job. I told him Frou-Frou wasn't going with me, I said it and looked somewhere else. Etienne didn't say anything and never mentioned it again. But for a long time I turned the idea around in my mind, I didn't even mention it to Frou-Frou; I hardly ever talked over my business with her, and if I did, it had to be very quiet, in the middle of the night or when we were alone, and that hardly ever happened because Carmelite was always around, complaining about how heavy her belly was, complaining about her husband Jean Pierre, complaining about all of us. When Paul left she complained even more, now she didn't have anybody to provoke.

It suited Frou-Frou and me that the youngest of my mother's brood had gone away with Etienne. Without Julien and Paul on the other side of the partition we could talk in bed and sigh and not worry about anybody hearing us. I began to stay with her till morning, and one day Carmelite came in and saw us together, I was sleeping with my arms around her mother, and she woke her mother to ask for some remedy. Frou-Frou moved my arm so she could get up and help her, but then she came back to bed and put my arm back where it had been, and that meant she didn't care if her daughter saw us. It also meant something else: I had spent the night with her and everybody knew that obliged me to take her as my wife. It scared me, and I lay stiff as a board in that bed, and Frou-Frou became very soft with me because she knew what I was thinking, she pressed against me, and it was late when we got up.

Julien came back to find that his half brother Paul had gone away to Côteaux, but that his half brother Thierry was still in the house and living openly with his mother.

"You didn't go to Port-au-Prince," he said.

They had given him a few days leave and he spent the time in his room, his lair, smoking a lot and drinking his good bottles of liquor and avoiding meals with the family. One afternoon two men came to see him, they left the house to talk. Julien had become more mysterious, I could see that he was older.

Three or four days later we heard about the massacre. In Gonaïves thirty-two corpses were found in a grave that had been badly dug and filled in even worse. People saw dogs carrying away the pieces and followed them until they discovered the jumble of arms and heads. Seven of the thirty-two were women, and two of them were pregnant.

"Julien is mixed up in this," said Frou-Frou.

But she never had the courage to ask him about it. Then they told Jean Pierre at work that the *macoutes* who had killed so many people in Gonaïves had come from Jérémie and then stayed a while in Port-de-Paix, looking for some other people they were supposed to kill too, but they never found them.

The money I earned with Papa Crapaud was running out, and Jean Pierre got me a job at the same warehouse where he had worked for so many years. I worked as a driver, I left early and picked up merchandise in those towns along the coast, they gave me a small truck and at night, after I unloaded, I drove the truck home so I could leave again the next day. The owner of the warehouse knew my house was also Jean Pierre's, that's why he trusted me.

One morning I left for Cayes, I was supposed to wait there for a shipment that would come by sea from Jacmel. The boat was a few hours late, and by the time I set out for Jérémie it was almost midnight; Jean Pierre was waiting at the warehouse to help me unload, and then we started back to the house together. That was where they stopped us, near the house, two men in uniform signaled for us to get out. We did, almost at the same time, Jean Pierre on one side and me on the other, and I started to take out my papers when I felt them grab me from behind, they grabbed Jean Pierre too but pushed him back in the truck and told him to stay there. They shoved me, backed me into a tree across from an open field and began to beat me, they kicked me in the head and they kicked me in the balls. Do you know what a man feels when he's kicked there? That's where his dignity is, at least that's what Papa Crapaud thought.

When they got tired they threw me on a pile of stones, lit cigarettes, and drove away in a jeep. Then Jean Pierre came to help me. He picked up his wreck of a brother and put him in the truck like a bundle, the way the husband had put his wife into the car when I brought her down from Casetaches, and when he reached the house he called for Frou-Frou to help him.

I was in too much of a daze to talk and it was Jean Pierre who told her what had happened. I hardly knew what was going on when they undressed me and bathed me in alcohol, applied hot and cold compresses, fed me a thick concoction that tasted of tobacco. Somebody, it turned out to be Carmelite, took pity on me and put ice packs between my legs.

The next morning I felt even worse. Every blow they'd given me hurt, all of them throbbing at the same time and in different places, and my head spinning, but I had my reasons for getting up at the time I always did. I dragged myself to the table and dropped into a chair. Jean Pierre and Carmelite didn't sit down, they stood in front of me to look at my face, it must have been the face of a ghost. Frou-Frou sat down, but once when I raised my eyes I saw that she wasn't looking at me, she was staring at the wall, staring as if she could see her whole life there; her eyes were very swollen, as if she'd been crying, swollen but dry, she wasn't crying anymore.

That's what the four of us were doing when Julien came in. He hadn't slept at home, nobody said so but I could tell by his clothes, he wasn't in uniform and his shirt was dirty and wrinkled. He went right to his lair, came back without a shirt, and sat at the table. Frou-Frou stood, brought a cup of coffee and put it in front of him, but kept standing beside her son. When Julien raised the cup to his lips, Frou-Frou hit him with her fist, she hit him in the face and the cup went flying, he looked at her in surprise, maybe it was fear, for the first time in his whole life his eyes looked like a child's eyes, but he didn't defend himself, it didn't occur to him that his mother would go on hitting him, and that's why the second blow sent him off the chair and the third knocked him to the floor. And that was where Frou-Frou fell on him and scratched and pounded his face, she pounded him so much that her fists were covered in blood, Julien's blood. I didn't have the strength to move, and I don't think Jean Pierre and Carmelite had the strength either; a little while before they'd been looking with horror at my ghost face, and now with the same horror they were watching Frou-Frou go crazy.

She got to her feet and went to the kitchen. Julien lay there facedown, he didn't moan, he just made some noises in his throat; he stopped when Carmelite began screaming, or maybe what happened was that her screams drowned out the noises in Julien's throat. My head was on fire and I couldn't move from my chair but I could see Frou-Frou's hand, she was holding a knife in that hand, holding it high, she attacked her own son again, and if Jean Pierre hadn't grabbed her at the last minute, she would have killed him.

The knife fell and Carmelite had the sense to pick it up and put it on the table next to my cup of coffee. Some neighbors came when they heard the screams, and a woman who lived next door took Frou-Frou home with her. Carmelite went with them, and the three men were left in the house, two full-blood brothers, that was Jean Pierre and me, and a half brother whose half-blood was spattered on the floor.

Jean Pierre helped him up and Julien went back to his lair, spent a while in his room, and came out carrying the same knapsack that Frou-Frou had packed for him when he left for Gonaïves. He still wasn't wearing a shirt, but he had put on his army boots, the laces were untied, maybe

that's why he dragged his feet a little. He passed us and
didn't look at us, didn't say a word, he left the door open
and went out into the world.

Frou-Frou didn't come back until it was very late;
Carmelite brought her back and took her right to her
room. That night more than ever I felt obliged to sleep
with her, I went there in silence and held her hand, but
neither of us slept. She cried almost till dawn and it hurt
me between my legs, my mouth was burning, I had lost
two or three teeth in the beating. The memory of my
father hurt me.

Nobody mentioned Julien again for a month, or a
month and a half, then one day when Frou-Frou was serving fish soup, she said to Carmelite:

"Today's your brother's fifteenth birthday."

I still remember that soup, it had nice soft chunks, and
the heads were on the bottom. Fish heads in soup always
look like they're laughing.

✕✧✕ T H I R T E E N ✕✧✕
Pereskia Quisqueyana

They found a body without a face hanging from a mango tree at the entrance to the village of Jérémie.

It was on the same day we arrived, at dusk: People were milling around the street and Thierry surmised it had something to do with a dead body, perhaps more than one; these days almost no one died alone, not in Haiti, not in this desolate land.

We got out of the car and what at first seemed the back of the head turned out to be the face, they had cut off the nose and flayed the skin from forehead to chin. The poor bastard had kept his shirt—he was naked from the waist down—and the flies swarmed angrily around his neck.

I heard Thierry say that for some time corpses had been mutilated in this way so no one could know who they had been in life, and by the time anyone did, it was too late. He recalled that when he was a boy he went out one morning with Paul to look for wood and came across something similar. Or rather, Paul told him he had found a tree that grew old shoes instead of fruit. The two of them went to see this wonder, and it was true there were shoes, you could see the black tips through the twisted branches, but farther up there were legs and ruined bodies too. He covered his brother's eyes so he wouldn't see the rest: the devastated, unrecognizable faces, without their noses, without their covering of skin.

Only Carmelite and her daughter Mireille still lived in the house where Thierry had grown up, a little wooden house that had been patched and patched again. Carmelite had been separated from Jean Pierre for over twenty years, her brother-in-law Paul had lived with her a long time but he had left too. Now Paul lived alone, though he came to eat with Carmelite almost every night; Mireille cooked for her uncle and her mother, who was almost blind.

I didn't ask what had become of Frou-Frou. When I saw her daughter looking so old, I assumed the mother must be dead. And I was right. Thierry took a photograph from the table and placed it in my hands: It was the half-faded photo of a somber woman with very thick lips and very thin eyebrows that had been tweezed into arches. She had a broad forehead and high cheekbones, so high they made her eyes look small. To have her picture taken she had put on a little hat with flowers, and probably had painted her lips, though I wasn't sure about that, the photograph was black and white and her mouth would have been prominent with or without lipstick.

"She died four years ago," said Thierry. "She became a little confused, she would see me and ask about Claudine, about the children. She thought I was my father."

He replaced the photograph, looked at it for a few seconds, and then went to another room and came back with two more pictures.

"This is Etienne's son," he said, handing me the first. "He's become religious. And this is my sister, Yoyotte." He handed me the second photograph. "That's her daughter with her, they still live in Bombardopolis."

Etienne's son hadn't wanted to look into the camera, he was standing sideways; the picture was small but you could see part of his white shirt and a dark tie, surely a black tie. Yoyotte was a tiny woman, completely different from what I had imagined, she looked like a little old lady but was a year younger than Thierry. Her daughter, on the other hand, was a tall, heavyset young woman with short, spiky hair; for the picture she had laughed and placed her arm around her small mother, tilting her head until her porcupine bristles touched the other woman's gray hair.

That night I slept in what had been Frou-Frou's room; Thierry rapped his knuckles against the partition, said that twice he had found termites, and mentioned that Julien and Paul had slept on the other side when they were boys and until they became men. Now on the other side there was a table with lengths of cloth, a fairly old sewing machine, and a chair. Mireille sewed for a living. According to Thierry she was the best dressmaker in Jérémie, she made wedding dresses, but not so much these days. She also sewed first communion dresses, fewer and fewer of those. They had called on her to dress the saints, she dressed all the saints in the Jérémie church. It would be years before they had to be dressed again.

Paul didn't come for supper that night, but he showed up for breakfast the next day, almost at dawn, when we were just finishing the packs we would take with us on our first expedition to Casetaches. He was still a young, robust man; in a way, he looked like Thierry's son though they were less than ten years apart. After we exchanged greetings, he sat down to watch us work, Mireille served him coffee and he had an affectionate word for her; I couldn't understand exactly what he said but I noticed that he looked at her with tenderness, with a father's uncomplicated glance. Then he turned back to us and told Thierry about new trails that would make it easier for us to climb the mountain. He paused, drank all his coffee in one swallow, then mentioned in a casual way that there were already two foreigners up on Casetaches looking for frogs.

Thierry raised his head, squatted next to the packs for a moment, then dropped everything and walked toward his brother. I also put down the flashlight I was checking and immediately went over to Paul, and only then did he realize he had said something very serious.

"Maybe they're not looking for frogs, but people saw them catch some. And birds and bats too. A woman and a man, and their guide."

He stopped, drank from his cup again, and was disconcerted to find that only a bitter sediment was left.

"What they mostly take is plants," he continued, "plants with thorns, the more thorns they have, the faster they take them. The woman has a camera and she takes a picture of the plants before she pulls them up."

Botanists, I was sure of it. Thierry asked his brother where the strangers were sleeping.

"When they're not on the mountain, they stay in Marfranc. The couple sleeps there, but not the guide. I don't know where the guide sleeps. I know his name is Luc, he's a Haitian from Port-au-Prince, or somewhere, but not from Jérémie."

Marfranc was a little hamlet almost at the base of Casetaches, it was, in fact, the last inhabited place we would see before we climbed the mountain. We planned to leave our vehicle there, the tomato-red Renault we had driven from Port-au-Prince; we'd leave part of our photographic equipment and some canned food in the car, and a family Thierry knew would take care of it. The plan was to bring up supplies gradually, go back and forth for water and food. I decided that the first expedition would be more for reconnaissance: finding and marking areas that we would search more carefully later.

We reached Marfranc at noon. The couple I had assumed were botanists weren't there, they'd gone to Casetaches the night before and no one expected them to come down for three or four days. We went to the cabin they had rented; it was locked but we found dozens of pots scattered around it, mostly cactus and succulents, as well as other species set into rocks. The neighbors used these plants as an excuse to tell us that the interior of the cabin was filled with them too.

Climbing the mountain was easier than I had expected, thanks to the trails Thierry's brother had advised us to use. We worked that afternoon and all the following day, marking the countryside and photographing caves and streams, little ponds and tiny depressions in the heart of the mountain, drainage areas rich in bromeliads, the frog's perfect habitat. On the third day, when we were placing markers around a pool where an old man in Marfranc remembered seeing the *grenouille du sang* a long time ago, we heard noises followed almost immediately by the murmur of voices. We moved a little to the left and first we saw the woman, who was practically on top of us, and then the man, followed by the Haitian guide, a husky black who looked at us with war in his eyes. We exchanged greetings and introduced ourselves. One of the botanists, Edouard, was French; the woman came from Iowa and was named Sarah. They both worked for the New York Botanical Garden and confirmed that they were collecting cactus, though the Frenchman's specialty was pollination, which was why they had been catching insects, birds, bats, but no frogs: It must have been some other animal that Thierry's brother had mistaken for a frog.

We agreed to meet the next day at their cabin in Marfranc. I told them I was tracking down an amphibian but didn't mention the species; they said they had seen few amphibians, just some toads near a stream on the north slope. The woman excused herself, saying she couldn't talk anymore, and moved away to dig in the earth. Thierry went over to her and I saw them exchange a few words.

That night, just before we went to bed, we listened to the radio. They mentioned the disfigured corpse we had seen at the entrance to Jérémie: They suspected it was the body of a schoolteacher who had been missing for five or six days. In addition to the mutilation of his face, the body was missing a finger, the index finger of his left hand. Thierry asserted that even though they didn't say so on the radio, the lack of that finger was like a message.

"The people in Jérémie know who killed him, and they know why they killed him."

I recalled a man who worked on my father's ranch and was missing a couple of fingers, he was a Vietnamese named Vu Dinh but my father called him Dino. He was in charge of the chicks, it was the only work he had ever done on the ranch, he had spent more than ten years with ostriches. When they were born the birds were very delicate, almost anything could kill them, sometimes they came out of the shell and refused to eat for three or four days, some never learned how to eat; others choked, died from so much pecking at the sand. Pneumonia caused the rest of the deaths. My father claimed that fewer chicks died on his ranch than in any other nursery in the country, but I never knew if that was true or not. The success belonged to the Vietnamese, and my father congratulated him often and patted him on the back.

"Do you remember what I told you about my brother Julien?" While he spoke, Thierry chewed on a small plug of tobacco. "He would leave his message too, his own mark on the dead man."

Vu Dinh, or Dino, had a strange relationship, I always assumed it was sexual, with the woman who tended the incubators. She was a fleshy blond who clenched her buttocks when she walked, as if that were the only way she could control the direction her body would take. I was there one afternoon when she handed Vu Dinh a box filled with newborn ostriches, casually mentioned that one of the chicks was lame, and told him its number—as soon as they were out of the shell she tagged them with a number—and he repeated it in a low voice, went on repeating it while he looked for the chick and finally took it out: He examined its feet, blew on its beak, and passed the three fingers of his mutilated hand over the yellow fuzz. Without giving it a second thought, he wrung its neck.

"The woman this morning," whispered Thierry, "was looking for signs too, but in the earth. She's looking for a plant that stands up on two feet when it rains. When the weather's dry it hides, like an animal, it folds up its legs and disappears."

My mother insisted that the fleshy blond was my father's girlfriend. She said this quite often, until one day I told her of my suspicions that she was really Vu Dinh's mistress. I remember her bursting into laughter: "Dino? You mean you don't know the little Chinaman doesn't like women? You mean your father hasn't told you?" And then she added: "You must be the only person who doesn't know, the husband is always the last to find out." It was a difficult blow for me to accept. I had been sitting next to her, and I remember that I stood up in a daze and left without saying good-bye. My mother called that night to ask if I was feeling better, but she didn't apologize, or mention the blond, or refer to Dad (she usually did), much less to Vu Dinh, or Dino, or the little Chinaman, as she called him. Before she hung up, she asked if Martha was home. I said she had gone to the movies. "With her friend Barbara?" I didn't answer, I dropped the receiver and left it dangling from the table, left it that way all night.

"The plant she's looking for"—Thierry again, in a voice so faint I wondered if he was talking in his sleep— "only grows on a mountain in Bánica, on the other side of the border."

We went down to Marfranc the next day and headed straight for the Renault, took out the rest of the equipment, and Thierry arranged new packs; a little while later he asked if he could go to Jérémie and spend the rest of the afternoon with his family. I suggested he ask again about the *grenouille du sang*, somebody must have seen it or heard it.

The people who were taking care of the Renault for us brought me some buckets of water so I could clean up. I shaved, and they sent for the man who passed for a barber in Marfranc, a scarecrow of a man named Phoebus, to give me a haircut. What he did was criminal, he left separate little clumps of hair all over my scalp, and I was tempted to tell him to shave my head but restrained myself—I thought all those little tufts were better than the scrapes and nicks he was bound to dispense with his razor.

Late in the afternoon I went to see the botanists. Edouard was there to greet me. He was alone, but in a little while Sarah came in, offered her hand (her skin was rough), and asked me to sit down. I had to climb over boxes and pots to find a space where I could sit, on the floor, naturally, all the chairs were covered with jars containing preserved plants, cactus, for the most part.

The first thing was to let them know what Thierry had said: The plant they were looking for, which my guide had described as a kind of remote-control cactus that comes to the surface on rainy days and buries itself again when it's dry, could only be found along the Dominican border. Thierry was from the area, I added, he had experience in this kind of work, and his advice was worth listening to.

"Well, as a matter of fact, that's not exactly what I'm looking for," Sarah replied. "It's complicated, I didn't want to discuss it with your guide, what did you say his name was?"

She poured me coffee from a thermos she had pulled from under a stack of papers. It was very bitter, and Edouard took some sugar cubes from his pocket and offered me one, but I refused and drank the coffee plain.

"I'm looking for the *Pereskia quisqueyana*," Sarah continued. "That's a cactus, there are only three or four left in the whole world, all of them male. We need a female specimen."

She lowered her eyes and stared at the jars covering the floor, and I took advantage of the pause to ask if they had been on Casetaches long, but Sarah didn't hear me, or didn't think the question important.

"It's been seen here," she said suddenly. She had short, yellowish nails and soil stains on her hands, I was familiar with those stains, I knew they didn't come off easily. "A man from Germont, that's a little village near here, described a plant that might be a female specimen. No botanist has ever seen one, we don't know what the flower or the fruit look like."

She would have been a beautiful woman if her eyes hadn't been set so deep. I estimated her age at thirty or thirty-five, who knows, she could have been twenty-seven or twenty-eight, the skin on her face was weatherbeaten, that happens to herpetologists too, we get burned on the nose, the forehead, the cheeks. Sarah still had a smooth mouth and a long, slender neck, that's where you could see her youth.

"And you, what are you looking for?" she asked in a friendly tone. "People don't risk coming to Haiti unless they're looking for something important."

"*Eleutherodactylus sanguineus*," I said. "It's a purple frog, not many of them left, and if there are any they're probably all male, like your *Pereskia*."

She wasn't very tall, she wore her hair pulled back, brown hair, rather ordinary. Again I thought it was too bad her eyes were so deep set, especially because of the shadows around her lids, dark circles that by this time must be permanent and didn't even have the charm of indicating fatigue or a bad night. Luckily, her nose was perfect.

"I've spent six years looking for it." Sarah's voice broke, she sounded almost desperate. "I've checked the DR, and the border, I was on Gonâve and went over every inch of that island. I've been to Grande Cayemite and Petite Cayemite. And something tells me it's here."

She looked at the Frenchman, who had been silent the entire time, listening to us and drinking his coffee. I don't know why she looked at him when she said the rest of what she had to say:

"Something tells me it's here. And I won't leave without it."

In 1930, explorers and mountaineers learned of the existence of a small amphibian with peculiar nocturnal habits; it was found in abundance above 14,000 feet in the Sierra Nevada de Santa Marta, in northeastern Colombia. This was the only animal in the world that "froze to death" at night and "revived" with the morning thaw.

Floating on its back beneath the water, its tiny mouth breaking the surface, the *Rana carreki* would freeze in the ice, its vital signs diminishing or ceasing altogether, with no damage to its internal organs.

In the 1980s there were reports of a substantial decline in the number of frogs observed in ponds along the Sierra. In 1992, a mountain climber, whose mission was to collect a specimen, returned from the Sierra empty-handed. Another search in 1993 also failed to produce results.

The *Rana carreki* is completely black. Those who have seen it state that the skin gives off a silvery glow.

✖◈✖ F O U R T E E N ✖◈✖
Secret and Greatness

Cameroon.

That's what the man's name was. Or at least that's what he said his name was. I met him on my first trip to Port-au-Prince, Jean Pierre and I had just turned sixteen, we saved some money and went on the little boat that made the crossing between Jérémie and the capital, it stopped for a while at Grand Goave, I think it stopped there.

The boat was called *La Saucisse*, not a common name for a boat—it was always crowded, crammed full of people, maybe that's why the owner decided to call it that. Jean Pierre carried a pack with two clean shirts, one for him and one for me. We were going there to have a good time, to meet women—in those days we had only fucked Carmelite—and to visit our friend Jean Leroy, he was a sailor on a schooner, and he lived in Cité Soleil. Jean Leroy's house was where we met Cameroon. And his wife, but we only saw her, we didn't talk to her. His wife was named Azelma, she was a light-skinned mulatta with sleepy eyes who always carried an iguana on her shoulder and talked like her tongue was sewn to the roof of her mouth.

Cameroon was a butcher. He was known as a good slaughterer, they would hold contests to see who could kill a cow, skin it, cut it up, and filet it in the shortest time. He almost always won, he had arms like a bull and hairy hands covered with scars, he could break a cow's neck with those hands. Even Jean Leroy, who was his friend, was a little afraid of him, it was terrifying to think of him angry.

The afternoon when we met him for the first time we hardly said a word, we didn't even dare to look at his neck—it was loaded down with necklaces—or his rings with the orange stones, or his leather wristbands studded with shells. Cameroon asked about our father, he had met him in Bombardopolis a long time ago, he wanted to know if Divoine Joseph was still alive, he burst out laughing and said Divoine was the only man who had touched his three balls—he was born with three—when he was a boy, to cure him of some sores he'd gotten from a woman. He also remembered what a good woman Yoyotte Placide had been in her youth, and he asked if my sister's godmother still had the food stand on the edge of town, he said it was the only place in the world where you could eat *djon-djon* made with cat liver. Then he told us something that Jean Pierre and I didn't know: The most famous cook in Bombardopolis, the protector of the *pwazon rat*, the spiritual mother of all the crews, had gone to bed with only one man, and that man was old Thierry, our father.

Silent, our eyes lowered, we heard something else too: It was because of Yoyotte Placide that old Thierry had killed a tracker from another crew. According to Cameroon, the tracker was drunk and tried to screw Yoyotte, nobody knew if he did, what they did know was that our father waited for him at the door, said something to him in a quiet voice, and cut him with the knife. The other man didn't try to defend himself, and old Thierry sliced him open.

When Jean Pierre and I came back from that trip we had changed a lot. Neither one of us spoke on the boat, we were thinking about what Cameroon had said. I remembered Yoyotte Placide's grief-stricken face when she heard that my father was going to have a child with Frou-Frou. Nobody thought anything bad back then, we didn't even suspect anything the time she said my father liked his bath nice and hot and his fish soup almost cold. My mother answered that maybe it was that way in Bombardopolis but in Jérémie his bath was icy cold and he liked his soup burning hot. Maybe Yoyotte washed my father's back or massaged his neck, who knows if it was to soften his heart, and licked his belly and didn't care about the soap. We were blind, and by the time we wanted to see, when we could see, Frou-Frou was in the way.

On my second trip to Port-au-Prince I saw Cameroon again. That was the trip I made to meet Papa Crapaud. A man came to Jérémie looking for a guide, I went to see the man and he said there were two conditions for the job: I had to know how to read, and I had to know every inch of Casetaches Hill. Then he tested me, he handed me a paper with writing on it and I read it out loud, then he asked me to draw the mountain, he told me to show the trails and the biggest caves. Finally he said I had to go with him to Port-au-Prince to meet the foreigner. The foreigner was the one who did the hiring, he was an old man who hunted frogs.

By this time *La Saucisse* didn't exist anymore, it had gone down near Gonâve. Now there was another boat, much bigger, and with a fresh coat of paint, it was called *Le Signe de la Lune.* The man and I got off that boat in Port-au-Prince and went straight to the hotel, where Papa Crapaud was waiting for us. He wasn't as old as I thought he'd be, he had a nice face, the hard smile of a man of the world, and those clear eyes, no little veins, no yellow crust in the corners of those eyes; he didn't know Ganesha yet, he hadn't slept yet in the arms of that rotten snake. He shook my hand and asked me to sit down, then he began to talk about frogs, he sketched a few on his little slate and asked me if I recognized them. Later he took out a photograph of a slimy toad all covered with warts, I knew the creature very well, we talked about its poison for a while and I told him what the fishermen in Jérémie always said, that this toad was the mother of all toads. Papa Crapaud started to laugh and said he felt like their father, that was when I thought "Papa Crapaud," and then I said it out loud. "You can call me that if you want to." He shook my hand again and told me to go back to Jérémie and find him a nice little house where he could keep his things. I was hired.

I left the hotel and started for Cité Soleil. On the way I bought a bottle of *clairin,* I thought I would ask Jean Leroy to come with me to celebrate my new job, celebrating for us meant doing a lot of fucking, taking a woman or two to bed. But Jean Leroy wasn't home, he was out in his schooner and it was Cameroon's wife who opened the door; she said hello in her phantom's voice and told me she usually stayed there when Jean Leroy was at sea. I could wait for her husband, he'd be back soon and would certainly want to drink that bottle with me. We were alone a long time but there was no danger because Azelma was pretty old and only cared about her iguana. When Cameroon came home I opened the bottle, he asked me what I was doing in Port-au-Prince, I told him about Papa Crapaud, and he gave me some advice. Then he talked to me again about my father, about the times they had been together in Môle Saint Nicolas, screwing the Dominican girls in one-armed Tancréde's cabaret.

Cameroon seemed to be an upright man, he began to seem that way to me when he lowered his voice to talk about "the Greatness," the secrets of men, the human seed of death. If I ever came to live in Port-au-Prince, he'd make sure I had a job and a path. The path of men, I remember him saying, lies in the Sacred Voice. I asked him what that Voice was, and he told me I'd find out one day.

That day arrived a few years later. Papa Crapaud was dead, and my wife, my wife was Frou-Frou, was gone from this life, and there was only one road for me to follow: I had to leave Jérémie forever, make my own life someplace else, which is what almost all my brothers and sisters had done except for Jean Pierre, who was stuck there because of Carmelite.

I didn't want to work as a butcher, much less a stevedore, I thought that was all Cameroon could offer me but I was wrong. He didn't offer me anything right away, he said he'd tell me a story that would change my life. He took me to a bar with mirrors on the Boulevard Allégre, it was very famous in those days, it was called the Samedi Night Club. He asked for *clairin* mixed with beer, and without tasting his drink he started to talk like a drunk-ard: "One says the river, just the river, as if there weren't so many in Calabar."

I didn't understand at first, but he went on saying strange names and talking about the Power reincarnated as a fish. Suddenly he opened his eyes wide and told me to shut mine: "Think about the woman, Thierry, about one, think about her as if you could see her." The woman was named Sikán and every morning she dipped a hollow gourd into the river for water. One day, when she pulled out the gourd, she heard the Voice, that full bellow, that trembling music deep inside it: She looked into the gourd full of water and saw the three-pointed tail. The wise men of Guinea got together, they locked Sikán away and took her fish, they skinned it and covered the mouth of the gourd with its skin. But it was no good, in its skin the Voice of the fish was only a weak echo of a Voice. Then they cut off Sikán's head, you worship with blood, with blood you waken the world, they put her head into the gourd, there her bird's eyes and the yellow eyes of the fish could look at each other, they sprinkled it all with the seven herbs, and finally the Blessing was heard: That was the deep drum of the Secret Society, the ancient drum whose name was never spoken, the Voice that is like the fire that warms the heart of the Abakuá.

Then Cameroon asked if I wanted to join the Society. I told him yes, as soon as I could, but that couldn't happen until I underwent many trials, trials of sorrow and trials of joy, which are the most difficult. They shaved my head, they took off my clothes so a man could paint my body, lines on my skull, lines on my arms and legs. Do you know who the man was who painted me? Emile Boukaka himself, you met him there in Port-au-Prince. Boukaka is the Mpegó of the Power, the Priest of the Symbols and Signs, the Master of the Casts, the Tracer of the Marks. He also put lines on other men that day; the signs create and rule, what is not marked is not sacred, not real. I was reborn under the Voice of Tanze, Tanze is the name of the Fish, but his head is called Añuma; his scales, Osarakuá; his teeth, Inikué; his tail, Iriama; his flesh, Abianke; and his waste, Ajiñá.

There were no women in the Society. There are none now and there never will be. A woman discovers the Secret, she may find it as Sikán found it, but then she must leave it, she must die, she must close her eyes. Do you see that countrywoman of yours who goes around pulling up plants on Casetaches? One day, when she least expects it, she will find what she is looking for, and I know very well she is not looking for the thing she says she is looking for, and then what will happen when she takes the female flower? A woman shouldn't be the one. Do you know what Cameroon told me? "The old ones always think that women lie."

Frou-Frou lied, she loved my father more than anybody else, a father who never called me by name, and because she loved the father she went to bed with the son. Claudine, my mother, lied to Yoyotte Placide, they were pious lies so we would go on having banquets, they talked to each other about how good my father was to both of them. Carmelite always loved my brother Paul, then she gave birth to that puny girl and said it was Jean Pierre's. She told a lie.

Cameroon didn't put me to work as a butcher or a stevedore. He found me a job in a tailor's shop, cleaning the floor and carrying messages, picking up the scraps of cloth, the pins and buttons that fell down. I met Amandine in the tailor's shop, though everybody called her Maude. The first time we were together she asked me if I had left a woman in Jérémie. I told her yes, sooner or later a woman is grief, the grief of Frou-Frou would last the rest of my life. I told her I carried her here; I still feel I am carrying her even though she's dead.

Later, Maude gave me a son. A man doesn't change because of that, Cameroon had already told me: a man doesn't change for anything. The child died soon after it opened its eyes, the midwife said it had come into the world with a broken heart. Maude cried for days, I thought she'd go crazy the way Frou-Frou went crazy, but then she started to calm down. She asked me if we could have more children, I promised her we would, we'd have a son with a healthy heart and call him Cameroon. But it was a girl and we called her Yoyotte, like my sister and my sister's godmother.

Cameroon was her godfather. My sister Yoyotte came from Bombardopolis to cook the baptism meal. We celebrated on a Saturday morning. At noon on Sunday Azelma came to tell me the news and for the first time her sleepy eyes were wide awake: Cameroon had run off with Yoyotte.

They didn't go to Bombardopolis. They disappeared for a few years. Old Yoyotte Placide, who was almost blind, came to Port-au-Prince to find her goddaughter. Nobody understood how they could fall in love and decide to leave in so short a time, but the men in the Society knew, Emile Boukaka knew, he received a postcard from Guinea, he received several, Cameroon asked him to tell me they'd had sons, two at the same time, identical albino twins, there's nothing more sacred in this world.

Yoyotte Placide died soon after. The food stand was closed for a long time, but the crews of *pwazon rat* passed by from time to time and stopped to remember those midnight banquets, the smell of beans that the cooks softened in *clairin*, the fried meat that some people said was black dog. Yoyotte said it was wild pig.

My sister and her two sons came back to Haiti, but Cameroon didn't come back with them. The children couldn't stand the light, albinos have their own brightness and the sun is a torment to them. She took over the stand again with the same name it had in the old days, Petit Paradis, and she began to cook the recipes she brought with her from Guinea. Later on she had a daughter, she had her with Gregoire Oreste, the man in my father's crew whose job it was to finish off the hunt. The girl still lives with her but not the twins, they have their own families; some women, and some younger sons who didn't come out so white, help her serve the food in Petit Paradis.

Sometimes somebody would pass through Bombardopolis and stop in to ask for Cameroon. Some said he died in the river Oddán, that he died of his own free will, going into the water with weights. Others claimed he fell in love with a blue girl in Guinea who bound him with her Power. Yoyotte told me the truth: Cameroon came back to Haiti long before she did, he came back to Azelma, his wife with the sleepy eyes, and they went to live in Agua Negra, a village on the border where nobody ever went. But Divoine Joseph went, he saw Cameroon and told Gregoire Oreste, that's how my sister found out, Gregoire wanted to test her and she stayed calm, nursing her little girl, she didn't even tell the twins, by that time they were asking about their father.

In the Society they said things a certain way. Not saying anything was also a way of saying. When they talked about "the Greatness" they lowered their voices, when they talked about Cameroon they didn't talk. They said everything in silence, as if he was dead, he must have died in Agua Negra, and his wife Azelma, too. But there are still those who see them. Yoyotte, my sister, says she has seen them in Bombardopolis, and she tells her twins, the albinos fathered by Cameroon, in a very quiet voice.

I am marked until death, what else can I say? When I die, on sea or on land, Cameroon will be there, my father too, Frou-Frou will be there if my father doesn't object. I will always be in debt to Cameroon for the Voice. Better if it happens at sea, that's where Tanze moves.

Soul of a *Macoute*

I recalled the postcards I had seen in Emile Boukaka's office. Most from France but some from unexpected places; who had ever been to Bafatá?

Cameroon, perhaps, that passionate, mystic butcher who could make himself invisible and then mix in with the crew on a freighter. A man, I suddenly thought, who brought to the slaughter a sense of a quest: He killed, skinned, cut up cattle with his mind fixed on their guts, their blood, the final destination of the shit they would never pass from their bodies. That must be why he won all the contests: For Cameroon, the slaughter was a road to perfection.

It's also possible he never set foot in Africa. In that case he might have run away to South America. I tried to remember what was written on the card I had read at Emile Boukaka's: "*De Pérou, une photo de mes chers anthropophages.*" It was an Indian hut in Beni, Bolivia, which means the sender was confused, or trying to confuse the recipient. Unless the postcard from Beni had been carried to Peru and sent from there, in which case it wasn't deception or confusion but simply a whim or an oversight.

In any event, Thierry's tale was meant to show how trustworthy the men of the Society were, because one of them, a member who might even have been Emile Boukaka, had given the warning: Casetaches would soon become a forbidden place, just like the Mont des Enfants Perdus, Gonâve Island, Carcasse Bay, and the towns of Tiburón and Port-à-Piment. Frog hunters and flower seekers would not be able to stay there much longer.

"Jérémie has been hell since yesterday," Thierry whispered, turning his back. "My brother Paul is leaving with Carmelite and Mireille, they're going to Bombardopolis to see if they can be safe there."

"We have food in Marfranc," I said, "we don't have to go back to Jérémie until we find the frog."

"The world isn't right for hunting frogs," Thierry replied, "least of all the *grenouille du sang*, it never lets itself be seen just like that."

The next day, late in the afternoon, we met up with the botanists again. We were near the cabin, packing the equipment, when we saw them coming toward us. I waved a greeting, Edouard stopped and Sarah kept moving, they were both carrying nylon bags on their backs and I could see she was walking with difficulty. They had spent the day in their "study quadrants," that's what they called the areas they had marked; they worked for as long as it was light, while we began when it was growing dark. Their canteens were empty and they asked us for water. I asked if they wanted to eat with us, they exchanged glances for a moment, and she accepted with a brief gesture, nodding her head and sighing deeply. I offered to carry her bag for her, Edouard came over to greet Thierry; he was a warm person, full of energy.

We opened some cans and ate, listening to the radio. From time to time Sarah made a vague or inconclusive remark. They had spent the day working on their own because Luc, their Haitian guide, was in Marfranc. I wondered for the first time if the two of them were a permanent couple or if solitude, fatigue, the tormented dry silence of the mountain brought them together only occasionally.

"I have no commitments," Edouard said suddenly, biting into a piece of boiled yucca; he was the classic type who adapts to everything, eats everything. "I would have liked to stay here for a couple more weeks, for Sarah's sake especially, to see if she can find her *Pereskia*."

Sarah looked up with a rather startled gaze, as if she were asking for my silence; silence about what?

"But it's going to be difficult," Edouard continued. "Luc told us it wasn't safe here. He thinks we could be killed."

Thierry cleared his throat. He was incapable of joining in a conversation if he thought it didn't concern him, but I could tell he wanted to say what he knew.

"They told Thierry that in a few days they'd force us to leave . . . Tell them, Thierry."

Sarah smiled, a genuine smile of battle. With a simple gesture she cut Thierry off.

"Well, we'll wait until they come for us." She spoke to her companion. "By the time they get here, we'll certainly have finished."

She was silent for the rest of the meal. Edouard talked about his wife and children. Sarah didn't speak again about anything or anybody.

That same night, and for the first time, we heard the call of what might have been an adult specimen of *Eleutherodactylus sanguineus*. Thierry heard it for a long time but I couldn't make it out; we went in and out of a cave, we kneeled for a while next to a tree, we followed a path around a small pond and suddenly he turned off his flashlight. It had rained that morning and now it began again. We stood there, not moving, we were on an uncomfortable slope and I tried to squat down but Thierry stopped me: That was when it began to sing again. I closed my eyes and heard it so clearly I wanted to shout. Then it all seemed very fast to me: I moved and slipped in the mud, Thierry turned on his flashlight and gave me his hand.

"That's the devil. Now we know it's here."

At that moment, and even afterward, for several hours, I couldn't say a word. We moved slowly, lighting the undergrowth, the clumps of bromeliad, the roots of trees. From time to time Thierry would stop and we'd hold our breath, but the frog did not sing again. Shortly before dawn we sat down and lit cigarettes.

"Do you know that albinos let you know they'll be albinos before they're born?"

It had nothing to do with anything and my head began to ache. Thierry opened a thermos and poured some hot coffee into an empty can of peas that still had its label.

"This is how they do it: They move a lot in their mother's belly, her belly becomes shiny and changes color. Then the mother, just to be certain, goes into a dark room, undresses, and stands in front of a kerosene lamp. If you can see the fetus from the outside, there's no question it'll be born albino."

I rummaged through my pack and took out two

aspirin. On my father's ranch they did the same thing, but with ostrich eggs: They would collect them, brush them off and wash them, and then hold them up to a lamp to find the yolk, which was a dark spot. Depending on where that spot was located, they would place the egg in the incubator. The spot always had to be on top. I helped them do this a few times, during summer vacation. I also liked feeding the chicks but avoided getting near the adult birds. I preferred to watch them from a distance, and sometimes I would see my father inside the corrals, moving like a bullfighter, trying to calm one that was angry.

"Yoyotte's children are very upright. Albinos always turn out that way: either very upright or very twisted, there's no middle ground."

When I was a boy I had a coloring book whose central drawing showed an ostrich race. The riders had beards and wore turbans and galloped without looking at one another, waving their sabers and raising a whirlwind of feathers. Somebody suggested I color the feathers yellow, perhaps it was my father, by that time he already had it in his head to breed ostriches. I did what he said, I colored the feathers and the riders' turbans, everything the same color, but even so, for a long time I had a desert nightmare: The ostriches were catching up to me and I was alone, caught in the whirlwind, my mouth filled with feathers, black, not yellow, and since my mouth was full I couldn't scream.

"One of the men outside Papa Crapaud's house, the ones who wanted to fuck Ganesha, was an albino."

My mother believed that raising birds was a waste of time and money: Who cared about ostrich feathers? How many feathers could my father get from a bird that would be so expensive in the long run? He answered that the profit was really in the meat: healthier than beef, more delicate than turkey. My mother shouted that they didn't have a single friend, relative, or acquaintance who had tasted or would even want to taste ostrich meat. My father lowered his voice: They will taste it, they will . . .

"He was one of the twisted albinos, a fat, savage man, but Ganesha opened the door to him, it was during one of Papa Crapaud's expeditions, and after he fucked her the albino beat her, he left her lying there in a pool of blood. I was the one who found her, much later, she couldn't move but she was praying in a whisper."

Then my father argued that there was money to be made from the skin, something like fourteen square feet of skin from each bird, ostrich skin brought a high price. But my mother wouldn't be convinced no matter what he said: Let him throw his money out if he wanted to, in the end it was all the same to her, but he couldn't touch her money or her son's.

"She spent several days in bed. Papa Crapaud took care of her even though he knew the albino had given her the beating, that he beat her because she let him fuck her. Ganesha was quiet for a time, and the albino disappeared. Later I found out he had killed two women."

Martha didn't want to go back to my father's ranch. Before we were married we went there fairly often, but later on, the ostriches stopped being a curiosity, at least for her. It wasn't unusual to drive down the highway and see them in the distance, on the farms, running; at that time there were a lot of ostrich farms in Indiana. Martha wasn't interested, any more than she would have been interested in a yard of chickens or a field of cows.

"He killed one in Jérémie and cut up the other one in Port-au-Prince. He pulled the skin off the face of the one in Jérémie, does that remind you of anything? I think that albino had the soul of a *macoute.*"

It was with Barbara, not me, that Martha ate ostrich meat for the first time. It was during a fast trip to Houston, Barbara wanted to have her heart checked, nothing very serious, an arrhythmia that bothered her at night. After some tests and a visit to the doctor, who was very reassuring, they went to a restaurant to celebrate. Martha said she saw ostrich filet on the menu and thought about me. She had never wanted to eat it on my father's ranch; before we were married she would bring her own frozen meals. But with Barbara she felt brave, or perhaps Barbara talked her into it, in any event, the fact that Martha ate ostrich with her and not with me was a subtle blow, the kind of fatal twist of the knife that stabs you in exactly the right spot, the precise nerve that will paralyze your whole body. That night they stayed in the hotel across from the hospital, a depressing place according to what she said later.

"Once I caught Ganesha eating frogs' legs. I told her if Papa Crapaud found out, he'd kill her. Her answer was that they were very good and her family in Guadeloupe always ate them."

I asked Martha if she had liked the ostrich and she said yes, it was pleasant, period, nothing special, less cholesterol, wasn't that the whole point?

"Papa Crapaud never found out, but sometimes she stole frogs from him and ate them. The albino joined her for the feast. After the albino left, it was the man from Léogane who kept her company."

My mother always blamed her separation from my father on "those damn birds." In spite of the years that had passed and the success of my father's business, she insisted he was an eccentric and the ranch an act of madness.

"Today is a great day," Thierry insisted, closing the thermos. "I never thought I'd be happy to hear the *grenouille du sang.*"

I never thought about the possibility that sooner or later the ranch would be mine. It was Martha who mentioned it one night: Since I was the only heir, had I investigated how hard it would be to sell an ostrich nursery? I looked her in the eye: "That depends." As always, she didn't look away: "Does it depend on the market or what?" My voice was a little hoarse: "It depends on me. I'll probably keep the ranch and all the ostriches."

"After we find the frog," said Thierry, "I'll save some money and go to see the birds. I don't know if your father will want to show them to me . . . "

Martha burst into laughter. I assume she told Barbara right away, and that Barbara also saw the humor. They laughed a great deal when they were together, they understood one another and had a good time together, and that's not easy.

"First I'll see them, then I'll find out if I can bring one here. Nobody's ever seen anything like it in Haiti."

I stood up and dusted off my clothes; the sun was beginning to bother me. Thierry waited for me to say something.

"Let's go to sleep," I said.

The waterfall frog, or *Rana cascadae,* was so abundant in the lagoons of southern California that until only a few years ago a single collector could find forty or fifty specimens in the space of half an hour.

In the autumn of 1992, an intensive search for the frog was carried out after reports were received of a serious population decline in its regular habitat, including the environs of Lassen Volcanic National Park, a protected area that has undergone no significant environmental changes.

Only two dying frogs were discovered.

The complete disappearance of the *Rana cascadae* is considered a fait accompli.

✕◈✕ SIXTEEN ✕◈✕
The Faith of Guinea

I see you're not fucking Frou-Frou anymore."

I didn't move or say a word, I couldn't. Julien looked so much like my father that I froze, standing there at the bar of the Samedi Night Club, the place with mirrors I'd gone to for the first time with Cameroon.

"You're my brother," I said.

"I don't have any brothers," he answered.

Much taller than any of us, I mean, my mother's children, much stronger too, Julien had the eyes of a vandal, who knows how to give orders, and a jawbone as big as a horse's. A man's strength is always measured by that bone.

"You're my brother even if you don't want to be."

I had just left Maude and was seeing a woman named Suzy, she was a nurse at the hospital in Port-au-Prince, or almost a nurse: She knew how to do some things and not others, but since the hospital was always too crowded, Suzy had to do everything. Julien noticed me because he noticed her first, I had my arms around her and he stopped to look at her, then he recognized me, came over, and then spit that filth at me.

"Aren't you interested in fucking Frou-Frou anymore?"

He wore a revolver at his waist and an olive-green shirt buttoned up to his neck, and a watch and a ring. I offered to buy him a beer but he turned away and went to sit at a table with two other men; every once in a while he'd glance over at us. Suzy asked how the children of the same father could look so different. I told her we were alike in one thing: We were both bald. You could see my whole scalp, and Julien had shaved his, he had a head like a bull, a broad, shiny forehead, he could have crushed rocks with it.

He never saw his mother. And he didn't want anything to do with any of his brothers or sisters. One time he was in Bombardopolis and went to eat at Petit Paradis. His friends were with him, the flesh and blood *macoutes* who'd replaced the toy soldiers in the game of *macoute perdu*. He didn't remember that the place belonged to his half sister, or maybe it didn't matter to him so much anymore. Yoyotte cared even less, because as soon as they came in, a little after noon, he and his men began to drink glasses of Barbancourt, and before it was dark there was a pile of empty bottles around the table. Then Yoyotte, my sister, called out the menu from the kitchen. Old Yoyotte Placide took care of waiting on tables.

"When Frou-Frou told you she was carrying me," Julien said to her with a big smile, "you wouldn't let her come to any more banquets."

Yoyotte Placide, who'd lived so long with the dead that she had lost her fear of the living, stopped to look at him, raised her voice, and answered very seriously:

"If it had been up to me, you'd never have been born."

My sister told me her knees turned to water. Julien's face went very dark, and the *macoutes* who were with him stopped laughing and listened to the conversation.

"You were too old," Julien said in a cutting way, "Thierry needed a younger woman."

He never called his father "father." Just to spite him and make him angry, he called him Thierry, then my father would hit him in the face, sometimes he split his lip. Julien didn't shed a single tear, he would lower his head and keep saying in a quiet voice: Thierry, Thierry, Thierry.

"You're the one who said it," replied Yoyotte Placide, "Thierry needed a woman, but what do you think your mother was?"

And he didn't call either of the women who had raised him mother. Claudine complained about it to Frou-Frou and Frou-Frou complained to my father. My father split Julien's lip again, he hit him hard, but he wouldn't stop yelling their first names: Thierry! Claudine! Frou-Frou!

"What was Frou-Frou, you crazy old bitch?"

Later my sister told me she almost burned to death that day. She was so scared she didn't know what to do while her godmother and half brother were arguing, and she began to turn round and round in front of the stove and knocked over a pan full of sputtering hot grease.

"I'll tell you what Frou-Frou was," Yoyotte shouted, the hatred of so many years eating away at her tongue, "she was a damn whore!"

My sister never knew what happened then because she fainted. When she opened her eyes she wasn't by the stove anymore. She was stretched out on two chairs, under the same umbrella where all the *macoutes*, with Julien in the lead, had begun to eat their stewed kid. Sitting beside her, fanning her with one of those fans that made such a nice cool breeze and had Papa Doc's picture on one side and the map of Haiti on the other, was her godmother, the loose-tongued Yoyotte Placide. The *macoutes* were talking, as happy as you please, they were laughing again, and they drank a lot more bottles, they didn't leave until late that night, when Julien paid the bill and said he was leaving a nice tip so the people would have enough *clairin* at the wake. He didn't say who the dead person was, he just threw the bills at the swollen feet of Yoyotte Placide.

That night at the Samedi Night Club, Julien wanted to settle accounts with me too. Maybe he was just trying to get Suzy, she wanted him too and stared at him with her mouth open. After he drank a while with his buddies, he came back to the bar and asked what was new with Frou-Frou.

"She got a little confused," I told him.

"She was confused when I was born. She gave me away to your mother."

And then, after he said that, he decided to finish with me: He grabbed Suzy by the arm and asked me if I would let her dance. He laughed when he said it and I didn't answer because I was waiting for her to do something, pull her arm away, or say no. But she let him take her, it all happened very fast, one minute they were together, dancing in front of me, closer together than any other couple, Julien had his hands on Suzy's backside and Suzy was moving with her eyes closed. I paid for my drinks and left, not because I didn't care about Suzy, I liked her a lot in those days, but I knew Julien was waiting for me to do something too, to make a move so he could kill me in front of everybody, kill me in cold blood.

Cameroon had already run away with my sister Yoyotte and Azelma, Cameroon's wife, would visit me from time to time to ask if I'd heard any news. Azelma had grown up in Port-au-Prince, she knew what was going on everywhere in the city, and she knew all about Julien. Who in Haiti didn't know about Julien Adrien?

One day she asked me if I knew how many people my brother's men had killed in the Cité Soleil massacre. I lowered my head: Azelma's revenge for Yoyotte running off with her husband was to tell me the truth, and the truth was that Julien stank of the devil, he not only killed men, but women too, a lot of them about to give birth, and he had killed children. Did I want to know how he did it?

"He's my brother," I remember telling her to make her be quiet.

And as soon as I said that I realized that when he died my father had left me all the faith of Guinea. What you loved, you had to respect. And what you didn't love but were bound to love, you respected that too. I didn't love Julien, how could I love a poisonous snake? But he was the youngest of my father's brood, and Frou-Frou's only male child, and I had to defend him or close my eyes.

"He's my brother," I said again, "and his mother is the woman I loved, the grief that will last forever."

Azelma was like a stone, but the time comes when even stones can understand what a man is saying. She didn't tell me any more about Julien or try to take her revenge for what my sister Yoyotte had done. We became good friends and I would comfort her, she'd ask if I thought Cameroon was coming back and I would tell her to be patient, any day now he'd walk in her door. And then she'd become thoughtful and run her hand along the back of her iguana.

Azelma didn't tell me, the men in the Abakuá Society told me: My brother Julien had joined forces with Cito Francisque, he's the man who controls the Mont des Enfants Perdus today. This was the time, a few years ago now, when the shipments began to arrive, the cargo they brought by sea and then sent on to the Dominican Republic. Cito Francisque and Julien had joined forces to defend their territory; another soldier was fighting them for it, a colonel who was connected in the Palace. The war began in Port-au-Prince, but then it spread to Cap-Haïtien; the dirtiest battle was in Jacmel. That's where the girl lived with her mother. I'm talking about Julien's daughter. He was in Pétionville, making plans with his men, when they brought him the package. They say he opened it, closed it again, finished giving his orders, and left with that package under his arm. He got into his jeep and disappeared for a few days. That's when he really went crazy. Julien shot men in the back of the neck, the back of the neck or the belly: He settled all his past and future accounts. That's why the Society wanted to warn me.

I didn't go to work for a few days. I hid in the house of Azelma's sister, a woman named Blanche, that's where I heard the news: They had seen the jeep in the middle of the night, they had seen it at the same time in Port-de-Paix and in Saint Marc. They had seen the wild man inside. Cito Francisque washed his hands of him, he made a deal with the colonel who was connected in the Palace, he gave him my brother's life, but it wasn't a life anymore.

One night Blanche came to my cot and said her sister Azelma had sent word: Julien had been killed in Gonaïves, they found him dead in his jeep, and they also found the package he was still carrying under the seat. It was his little girl's clothes, and her fingers, they sent him her fingers to prove they had killed her.

And then I didn't think about the beating he ordered when I began to make love to his mother, or his rage when he pulled Suzy away from me in the Samedi Night Club. I thought about the day he came to my house in the arms of his sister Carmelite, and my father told Jean Pierre and me, because we were the oldest, that the baby was also our brother.

Blanche put her hand on my head and said that now I could rest easy: The devil had gone to the devil. I took hold of her hand and put it to my mouth and began to cry, softly, not for the dead man but because I had to go to the wake and see Frou-Frou again. I got up from the cot and began to put on my clothes. Blanche sat there and watched me and said she wished Julien had never died. It was her way of saying she was sorry I was going and that I could stay, her way of offering herself as a woman, something she hadn't done for all the days I'd been hiding. I went to her, put my arms around her, promised I'd come back.

And I did come back to her house, but I brought Frou-Frou with me.

✖◈✖ SEVENTEEN ✖◈✖
Water in the Mouth

That night, before going into the field, I wrote two letters: one to my father, the other to Vaughan Patterson. The one to Patterson, which was supposed to be brief and dispassionate, turned out fairly long and somehow full of emotion. I told him I had heard the *Eleutherodactylus sanguineus* at last and could state with certainty that the frog was on the southern slope of Casetaches Hill. I hadn't seen it yet, I didn't know if I had heard an isolated specimen or several individuals from the same colony. What I could guarantee was that I would bring it personally to his laboratory in Adelaide.

The letter to my father was totally different, I wanted to be affectionate, I began by telling him about Thierry and his great interest in ostriches. It was a way of telling him that I was thinking about the ranch and the birds, that I often thought about him. But the letter came out so cold that I began another one, and then a third, and finally tore up all three. I made a little heap of torn paper on the ground and then kicked the pieces away with the toe of my shoe. That's when I remembered Oscar, the little stuffed ostrich my father had given me to help me get over the desert nightmare. It was white, as I recall, a sad-looking little animal with two big blue buttons for eyes and a tiny bow around its neck. My father invented a word game based on the name "Oscar the Ostrich," and urged me to repeat it every time I had bad dreams. The memory gave me an idea: I took a blank card from the supply I used for my files, wrote down the word game my father had taught me, and put it in an envelope addressed to him.

Just then Thierry came to tell me the equipment was ready; we were taking a tape recorder and three extra microphones that we would use in our attempt to record the voice of the *grenouille du sang*. I said we would go down to Marfranc the next day for water and food, and pay the man who was watching the car to take our mail to Port-au-Prince. Thierry looked at the scattered pieces of paper; I don't know if he realized they were letters I had torn up, or if he suspected that I had spoken of him in those letters.

"You still haven't told me how they kill the bird."

The first time I saw an ostrich killed—its head was cut off—I thought it was a simple, painless death. The head rolled to one side while the limp worm of a neck, still joined to the body, continued to move for a moment. Vu Dinh, or Dino, the Vietnamese who worked for my father, showed me that the bird's eyes could still follow an object for a few seconds even after it had been decapitated.

"If they have a neck," Thierry observed, "it must be easy to cut off the head."

Dino made necklaces, carved crosses or buffalo heads, from the shells of infertile eggs. He painted Vietnamese words on the necklaces, delicate markings that looked a little like decorations, but the woman who tended the incubators told me the words had a meaning, the words were curses.

"A hundred pounds of meat." Thierry sighed. "One cut to the neck and you have a hundred good pounds of meat."

The frog did not let us hear him that night. Thierry was impatient, he was concentrating on sounds, he spent a long time with his ear down to the ground. Finally he got to his feet, walked about fifty meters, and dropped to the ground again, pawing among the stones, shaking the bushes.

"It's close by," he said, "I can smell it."

Apparently the little amphibian could also smell us. It was a long, tiresome night. Thierry's impatience proved to be contagious, and we argued in whispers: He even suggested that the *grenouille du sang* was hiding because of my helmet, a comfortable helmet with an attached light, but he maintained that the beam was too bright and frightened away the frog. He said Papa Crapaud never wanted to use that kind of helmet, for one thing because it attracted moths around the face. He didn't stop grumbling until the sky began to lighten, it seemed to me he was interpreting the frog's absence as a personal failure, and I tried to explain that amphibians always behaved this way, immobility was a form of survival for them, as it is for us; immobility and silence, silence and perplexity.

Later that morning we returned to camp. From a distance we could see two figures waiting in front of the tent.

Edouard and Sarah were both staring up toward the top of the slope but didn't see us until we emerged from the bushes, when we were practically next to them.

"We're getting out," Edouard shouted. "They killed Luc."

It took me a few seconds to place Luc. Then I remembered that he was their guide, the man who'd looked at us with war in his eyes the first day we all met on Casetaches.

"They hung him in Marfranc," he went on, "and now they're coming for us."

I tried to catch Thierry's eye but he hurried into the tent without saying a word. I was beginning to understand his edginess, his vague insistence on finding the frog the night before. A member of the Secret Society had given the warning: Very soon Casetaches Hill would become a forbidden place. What Thierry hadn't passed on was the date, exactly when they'd begin to clear it out, perhaps tomorrow, or maybe in the next few hours, or minutes. Luc's death was a warning, a sign that we should all leave.

"He didn't have any feet, they cut them off at the ankles." Edouard walked up to Thierry. "Why do you people always have to cut a part off every corpse?"

Thierry opened his mouth, his face drenched in perspiration:

"Why should I tell you?"

We decided to go down to Marfranc together. We arrived there in the afternoon and the village was quiet, a fierce kind of quiet, nobody raised his eyes to look at us, the sky was overcast and I thought I could hear thunder somewhere, maybe in another world. Luc's body had been cut down, and the man who took care of our car offered to drive the remains to Port-au-Prince. Edouard insisted on going along, I decided to give him my correspondence, and the three men left in the Renault: two of them alive and one dead, a dead man without any feet.

Thierry walked around the village to find out the news. Sarah and I waited for him in a nameless café, a ghostly shack that sold only warm beer and homemade *clairin*. The place was small, and there were very few customers at that time of day: two men at a table, drinking in silence, and a couple dancing to music from a cassette radio. She was almost a child, twelve or thirteen years old I thought, maybe younger; he was a filthy, decrepit old man who stank of urine and took his dancing very seriously, clenching shut a wrinkled mouth that was surely missing some teeth.

The men who were drinking and not talking shot us a sideways glance when we came in. Sarah ordered *clairin* and then spent her time observing the strange couple; the music came in waves, some kind of French cha-cha-cha. When it was over, the old man went to sit down and the girl followed him. They both ordered beer and drank without speaking, the watchword seemed to be silence. I looked at Sarah, and she stared at her glass, a cloudy glass chipped around the edges.

"I'm about to find the *Pereskia*," she said. "Can they really make us leave now?"

"They already forced me off another mountain," I answered, "right outside Port-au-Prince, it's called the Mont des Enfants Perdus."

"Nobody's ever seen the female flower"—Sarah was a single-minded woman—"and nobody knows the color of the fruit, though I doubt very much that it's red."

"At the beginning of the last century," I told her, refilling her glass, "a white witch came to Port-au-Prince; she was very pale and was seen vomiting blood. I'm sure she was a hemophiliac, but they called her a *loup garou*, a kind of vampire. She set up a community on the mountain, brought fifty or sixty orphans with her, and taught them her magic. Nobody interfered, nobody cared about those children. Sometimes they came down from the mountain and went around the city in a group, people began to fear them, the children had become antisocial and unpredictable, sort of crazy."

Sarah looked at the old man again: The girl had her arms around him and was kissing his forehead and caressing his hair; all he did was chew at nothing with his puckered mouth. His stench reached all the way to our table.

"There were some girls in the group. Eventually they all became pregnant, some of them passed out on the street but nobody would help them, in Port-au-Prince they were more frightened of the females than the males."

The girl searched out the old man's lips and kissed them. I never thought I would find other people's kisses disgusting: There was a noise of lips smacking and a thread of saliva hung for a moment, connecting their mouths.

"One night there were bonfires on the mountaintop, and none of the children was ever seen again. The witch came down to Port-au-Prince and took the first ship back to France; nobody stopped her, nobody asked her about the children. The mountain used to have a different name, but from then on everyone began to call it the Mont des Enfants Perdus."

Sarah was about to ask me a question but she stopped

and gestured toward the door. There was Thierry, staring straight ahead, holding himself stiff, looking morose. I stood and walked over to him.

"My brother Paul didn't show up," he said. "Carmelite and Mireille couldn't go to Bombardopolis."

I asked him to sit with us. The two men who were drinking in silence got up and left; the old man was leaning on the girl, he had passed out or was too drunk. She seemed a little out of it too, staring into space with big, half-closed eyes.

"If Paul didn't show up, it means he must be dead."

Thierry also smelled of sweat; he moistened his lips with the tip of his tongue and I thought he'd ask for beer. But he ordered *clairin*, a double, a large glass that he raised to his mouth and emptied as if it were water.

"If you're going to get out," he said very slowly, "you have to do it now. Cito Francisque, the same one who cleared the Mont des Enfants Perdus, is coming here to clear out Casetaches."

Sarah looked at the ceiling, looked at the peeling walls, concentrated again on her glass, acted as if the warning had nothing to do with her.

"If you two don't leave, I don't know what will happen. Maybe they'll let you live, maybe they'll kill you and chop off a piece of your bodies. The piece they cut off will tell which gang did the killing."

"I can't believe they'll kill us," Sarah stammered. "They'll order us off the mountain, that's all. We have to stay. What harm are we doing up there?"

The girl who was with the old man stood up to get another drink, then she walked around the tables for a while, as if she found it hard to sit down again. I observed her carefully, she was energetic, muscular, a little black girl accustomed to hard work. She noticed me just then, caught me looking at her, and for a moment had the illusion that I was interested in her, but then she saw Sarah, a white woman with untidy hair sitting next to a tired, confused white man. She thought we were a couple and looked away; she was used to losing.

"Go up if you want to," Thierry said, "but do it fast, the faster the better."

I was worried by his tone and the distance he was assuming. I had the impression he would not go back with us. He may have decided to stay in Marfranc or return to Jérémie or find out where his brother Paul had gone, or what had been done to him. Perhaps he'd take care of getting Carmelite and Mireille to safety, maybe he was going to escape with them to Bombardopolis.

"I don't understand why you want to stay here," Thierry mused, suddenly noticing the girl, who had gone back to the old man and was regarding us with a certain sadness, "though they say that people don't die where they want to but where they have to, where their spirit seizes them."

The music started again, another French cha-cha-cha with a catchy chorus: "*Je t'en prie ne sois pas farouche, quand me vient l'eau à la bouche.*"

"We're staying," I told Thierry, putting my hand on his shoulder. "If you want to go back to Port-au-Prince, I'll understand."

He had stopped perspiring. The *clairin* had calmed him, and from the depths of that calm he looked at me with blurred eyes, as if we were all under water.

"I asked for my money in advance. I'll go up with you, but I don't know how we'll get down."

"With the *grenouille du sang*," I said. "We'll come down with the frog. And if we get to Port-au-Prince alive, I swear I'll give you an ostrich as a present."

"The bird," Thierry murmured.

Sarah was calmer too, and smiled for the first time in a long while; it was a beautiful smile, full of concern.

"Did you say an ostrich?"

In 1992, four frog species disappeared from Casuco National Park in Honduras.

Eleutherodactylus milesi, Hyla soralia, Plectrohyla dasypus, and *Plectrohyla teuchestes,* whose populations once abounded in the region, had given no prior indications of problems in the habitat, or any signs of decline.

The frogs disappeared without a trace, and not a single tadpole of the four species could be found in any of the numerous bodies of water in the area.

Biologists have emphasized "the catastrophic, unexplainable nature" of these disappearances.

❈❖❈ EIGHTEEN ❖❈❖
Cité Soleil

I lied to Blanche. I told her Frou-Frou was the woman who raised me when my mother died. Blanche believed it because Frou-Frou didn't look like anything else, she was dry now, she had changed. At Julien's burial, when we left the cemetery, she took me by the hand and asked me to take her far away, to a pretty place she could remember when it was time for her to die. She had never left Jérémie, the only pretty thing she could remember were those family banquets, and even the banquets had come to a bad end. That's how I got the idea of taking her to Port-au-Prince. I asked Carmelite to pack a suitcase for her, and we traveled there by sea.

Le Signe de la Lune, the big boat with the fresh coat of paint that I sailed on when I went to meet Papa Crapaud, it wasn't there anymore, I don't know if it went down or if they took it to Cayes; the boats leave Cayes and carry passengers to Jacmel. Now they had a mail boat called *Yankee Lady*—I always notice the names of boats and wonder why they're called what they're called—a noisy old

158

wreck that looked like it could never go anywhere. That stretch of sea between Jérémie and Port-au-Prince has a different color from the other seas I know, it gets rough in a different way, it has a thin, yellowish foam that looks like the foam on piss or bad beer.

I went on board very early with Frou-Frou. If you got there late you had to make the crossing holding onto the poles on deck, or up on the roof, or down in the hold, a hell with no windows that stank of animals. The breeders going to Port-au-Prince to sell their wares paid a little more so they could travel up above and tie their goats down below, or put their cages of chickens down there or their brown devil pigs, all the animals down there together, along with a few people who couldn't find anyplace better.

We went on board and found two seats facing the sea. Frou-Frou's suitcase was at my feet. She wore white shoes, she had put on an ironed dress and a little blue hat, and the hat had a piece of veil that covered half her face, you could see through the veil, I could see her eyes. Instead of the small black purse I had seen at the wake, she carried a big tote bag with her name embroidered on it, and she put that on her lap.

We were quiet for a long time, then I took her hand and said that in Port-au-Prince I wanted her to see the big, famous hotel where I met Papa Crapaud; they had a green piano there, and at night a woman sang, her name was June and she took off her shoes and sat on the green piano. Frou-Frou asked if I had a woman in Port-au-Prince and I told her about Maude, about the boy who had died and the little girl who was called Yoyotte. A puny little girl who was always sick. Then I told her about

Suzy, the nurse who knew how to do some things and not others but who had to do everything in the hospital in Port-au-Prince. I didn't tell her that Julien took her away from me one night, you have to let the dead rest in peace. Finally I confessed that of all the women I had known, Blanche was the one who reminded me most of her. We lived in her house. I explained that I didn't have my own house because I'd moved around so much after I left Maude: Some days I stayed with Jean Leroy, some days I was in the house where Suzy lived with her mother, and when it was all over with Suzy I went back with Jean Leroy again. Now I was with Blanche, and I thought the two of them would get along very well.

"Does she know you slept with me?"

"She knows you're like my mother."

Frou-Frou lifted the piece of veil hanging from her hat and looked at me in a rage.

"Men don't screw their mothers."

She dropped the veil and turned toward the water. There were other boats anchored near the *Yankee Lady*, a lot of rowboats, a naked man was cleaning out one of the rowboats with buckets of water. Frou-Frou sat and watched him; the man had arms as long as snakes and a round turtle head, a head too small for his stevedore's body. After a while we saw him turn to the side and piss into the sea.

"In the old days," said Frou-Frou, "what I liked best was to watch men pee."

I didn't say anything. The man in the boat shook off his privates and went on cleaning with buckets of water.

"The night your father sent you up to Casetaches, I saw a man pee and it drove me crazy."

I looked the other way, at the dock and the vendors coming on board with their baskets. The boat was filling up with passengers. A woman sat down across from us with her children.

"It was the man from Port-au-Prince who came with the foreigner. In the middle of the night I heard noises outside and I looked out the window, I thought it was him and I went out with a flashlight, I found him in front, wetting the grass. He asked me to turn off the flashlight and he didn't let me turn it on again until daybreak, and I went to wake you so you could go up to Casetaches."

I sucked in air with my mouth open, sometimes you have to suck in the air like that, swallowing every bit of air that will fit inside. One of the babies across from us, a little girl, began to cough. I thought about my daughter Yoyotte.

"The foreigner and the man from Port-au-Prince spent the whole day walking around Jérémie. You were up on the mountain, looking for the crazy woman on Casetaches, and your father was far away, in Saint Louis du Sud, somebody around there hired him. At night your brothers and I ate with those men. The foreigner didn't want to talk to us and he just lay there on his cot, but the one from Port-au-Prince played a while with Julien. In the middle of the night he came to your father's bed and lay down with me, I told him your father might come back in the middle of the night, and then he said we should go outside. We went out and I asked him to pee so I could watch him. He asked me whether I didn't want to go with him to Port-au-Prince, I could watch him pee every day there. In the morning your father came back and got into bed, the bed was cold because I had spent the night outside. He came back wanting to fuck and then I couldn't go to Port-au-Prince."

The boat siren sounded three times and still there were a lot of people coming on board, pushing to get on, they were stuck there, one foot on the boat and the other on the dock, and they were shouting insults at each other. A chicken fell in the water and a man jumped in to get it, he pulled it out half drowned, gasping, dripping oil. Frou-Frou may have been dry, she may have looked different, but her lips were the same as always, very tasty, with a lot of lipstick, and I felt my own rage and my dead father's too because that Haitian from Port-au-Prince had fucked her as much as he pleased. And to make it worse, the foreigner paid that Haitian good money to help him talk to my father.

"Your father fucked all the women. Did you know he fucked your mother and Yoyotte Placide and then they told each other about it?"

I nodded yes. Frou-Frou began to sweat, I saw the drops on her face and asked if she didn't have a fan. She opened her bag and took out a very old one, the one with Papa Doc's picture on one side and the map of Haiti on the other, she gave me the fan, and instead of fanning myself I started to fan her.

"Another time Carmelite's father came. You were with Papa Crapaud, looking for frogs. Your father, like always, was in Bombardopolis. I was alone in the house, alone with Carmelite, and her father came to see if it was true we were living with Thierry Adrien. He stayed a while and asked for a drink of water. Then he sent Carmelite to buy him some cigarettes, and then he forced me, in your father's bed, he wanted us to do it. I didn't tell him your father could come back any time because what I wanted was for him to come and cut him once and for all. But your father didn't come, and he finished, very happy, and got up to smoke the cigarettes Carmelite had brought him."

The heat eased as soon as we were out at sea. Frou-Frou stopped talking, and the little girl sitting across from me vomited into her mother's lap. I felt like vomiting too, I stood up and went to the railing, I leaned over the water and threw up the coffee I'd had for breakfast. When I came back, Frou-Frou gave me a handkerchief to wipe my mouth.

"I saw you pee once. You peed for a long time, you were thinking."

I gave her back the handkerchief. Frou-Frou smiled.

"That was after your father died. That's why I said I would wash your clothes."

I smiled too and put my arm around her. We looked like husband and wife. A husband with a wife who could have been his mother.

"You were the last man I saw pee."

She raised her head to look at me and I gave her a kiss on the lips, no matter how skinny and dry she was, those lips were still plump and purple.

We got to Port-au-Prince in the middle of the afternoon and went to Blanche's house. They got along from the beginning, they talked a lot about me and that made me happy. At night I slept with Blanche. I knew Frou-Frou was on the other side of the partition and I tried not to make any noise, and Blanche, who was a decent woman, tried not to make any noise either. One afternoon I told the two of them to fix themselves up, we were going to the Oloffson Hotel to have a drink. Blanche asked if I was sure they'd let us in, I said everybody there knew me from the days I traveled around with Papa Crapaud. Frou-Frou didn't look so dry that day, she put on another ironed dress and we walked the streets of Port-au-Prince until very late. When we got back to the house, Blanche wanted us to open another bottle, she was high and wanted to go on being high. Frou-Frou, stumbling over her words, said she wanted to tell me something, she could die any day now and it was right for me to know the secret. I broke into a cold sweat and looked at Blanche, I was afraid Frou-Frou would talk about us, but that wasn't her secret, it was about Carmelite. The girl Carmelite had with Jean Pierre, that Mireille who'd been born so skinny, she wasn't Jean Pierre's child but my brother Paul's.

"That doesn't change anything," I answered, very relieved. "She's still my niece."

"Someday somebody has to tell him," she insisted. "I want you to tell your brother."

I promised I would, though I was never sure what I should tell to which brother. Finally we all laughed and had a drink to celebrate that piece of news.

Blanche did sewing too, and she had a lot of free time, that's why she went out sometimes with Frou-Frou, she took her out when I was at work, they would go out and buy some cloth and have a beer. Between the two of them they sewed me a shirt the color of the *grenouille du sang*, I had always wanted a red shirt.

The night before Frou-Frou went back to Jérémie, we went to the Samedi Night Club to celebrate. The place wasn't so elegant anymore, Boulevard Allégre wasn't a very lively street either. The mirrors at the bar were broken, and the people who went there were different. I was careful not to mention Julien, there are dead men who can't rest. I danced with Blanche, and Blanche, who was a good woman, said to me: "Dance with your mother." I put my arms around Frou-Frou, I mean I put my arms around her bones, and even her bones reminded me of things. She could feel it and I heard her ask why I didn't come back to Jérémie; I held her a little tighter and said it wasn't the place for me anymore. The next day I didn't let Blanche come to the port with us, I left early with Frou-Frou, my excuse was getting a good seat on the boat, and I took her to Cité Soleil, to Jean Leroy's place, his house was empty.

"I knew we weren't going to the boat," Frou-Frou said. "Do you think a man screws his mother?"

A woman's bones don't change. Neither do a man's. We did it with our bones that day, they wanted to get out of our bodies and mix with one another and die there. And they did: Frou-Frou didn't move, I couldn't move either, but I had to. Without opening her eyes she grabbed my arm and asked me where I was going.

"I have to piss."

She held me tighter, she had a mouth that didn't need a thing, she ruled me with that mouth.

"Do it here."

When we finished, she still had time to get on the boat, and she wanted to leave. I promised I would go to see her in Jérémie, and I did, many times, until she was so old she began to mix me up with my father and ask me about Claudine, who was my mother, and her five babies, she meant me and my father's other children. She never asked about Julien, I think she erased him from her soul.

I had my third child with Blanche. It was a boy, and

since the first one had died, and the second one, my poor little girl, was about to die, I thought it over for a long time before I gave him a name. Blanche wanted to call him Thierry, and I told her that name would bring him bad luck. Then she wanted to name him after her father, his name was Henri, but the old man already had a lot wrong with him, I didn't want my son to suck in his sickness along with his name. I called him Charlemagne, it always seemed like a real man's name to me, it was the name of Yoyotte Placide's half brother, the one who prepared poisons in Gonaïves.

One night, a little while after Charlemagne was born, Maude sent for me because our daughter Yoyotte, who wasn't even four years old, had died in the hospital in Port-au-Prince. Blanche came to the funeral with me, I met Maude's new husband there, he seemed like an upright man but I didn't shake hands with him. You don't shake the hand of a man who dirties the plate where you've eaten no matter how upright he is.

After a time I made Blanche pregnant again; she stopped her sewing, and her belly began to grow big and high. I hoped she'd give me twins, the midwife said there might even be three, but that Blanche was very old for so many babies. Two days before the twins came into the world—one was alive, the other came out dead—the Society sent for me and ordered me to kill a man. Since I have the lines, I had to obey. The man was named Paul Marie, and I did it with a knife. Nothing else was ever used to settle the Society's accounts. You worship with blood and with blood you waken the world. I changed a lot after I did the killing. That changes a man, it surely does.

✕✕✕ NINETEEN ✕✕✕
Breakfast at Tiffany's

Sarah collected her gear and moved in with us; we would share the same tent. I wasn't sure if Edouard could get back. Thierry had heard that the roads between Jérémie and Marfranc were closed, there were soldiers everywhere and they weren't letting people through, soldiers were converging on the mountain and would begin the ascent very soon. We estimated that we had enough supplies for four or five days, and in that time we ought to find the frog, and Sarah, her cactus, her female specimen of *Pereskia quisqueyana*, her absurd female hiding somewhere on Casetaches.

She got up at dawn, just at the time we were returning to camp. For two days we would meet for a breakfast of instant coffee and crackers, and for supper, when we ate a pancake made of cassava flour, and sardines packed in oil. I was grateful they were in oil. I can't stand sardines in tomato sauce. The Vietnamese on my father's ranch—Dino, Vu Dinh—used to eat them every day. No matter what food they served, Dino would open a can of sar-

dines. In the summer we would all sit at the table on the
gallery that faced the corrals; my father always had lunch
with his employees, and I ate with him during vacation.
Unfortunately there wasn't much variety in the menu:
ostrich filet with vegetables, ostrich stew with squash, car-
rot and ostrich pie. Never chicken or fish, never beef.
Only what he grew on his ranch, he wouldn't give an inch
to his competitors. Dishonest competitors, my father
alleged, who took advantage of the public's lack of imagi-
nation.

The blond who tended the incubators sat next to Vu
Dinh and stole bits of sardine from him. There was a red-
headed boy, a voluntary mute who helped clean the corrals, who sat beside me. Then the old man who took care
of the storehouse, and two men, two brothers, who did
the hard work with my father: feeding the adult birds,
changing their water three times a day, roping them when
it was necessary, throwing them down so the veterinarian
could examine a neck, a beak, a foot that was weak, and,
of course, the crop. You never knew what to expect from
an ostrich's crop.

"Wait," Thierry whispered. "Please God, that's it."

It was our third day on the mountain, the third in the
last round of field trips, there wouldn't be any more. We
had just left camp, we had walked only about twenty minutes and found ourselves in an area that didn't seem suit-
able for any frog, least of all the *grenouille du sang*. It was a
fairly dry slope, with no grass or bromeliads, and I
thought that Thierry's longing to finish with the hunt was
making him hear things.

"Please God . . ."

It was dusk and there was still some light, a placid,

buttery light that slipped slowly among the trees and melted into pools on the ground.

"I can smell it," Thierry said again. "We'll have to wait till dark."

"It can't be here," I said. "The vegetation's not right, we'd better go higher."

"It's lost its way, but it's the devil. I heard it, sir."

I leaned against a bush to rest, and belched up the taste of sardines. After we were engaged, Martha came to the ranch with me one summer but stayed only ten or fifteen days; she helped me wash the ostrich eggs, soaping and scrubbing them with a good deal of skill. She said it was like washing dishes, not eggs. The woman who tended the incubators, that efficient blond, ignored her. She gave me instructions to pass on to Martha, whom she saw as an intruder, a typical, frivolous coed who comes to the ranch like a good little wife, ten paces behind her man. That wasn't my description, my father used it after Martha left. He showed me the newspaper clipping with our photograph and an announcement of what was called our "betrothal," he asked if I didn't find it embarrassing and I said it was all the same to me. Martha's grandmother, a punctilious woman, had sent in the picture and a brief note, and that's where we ended up, on the society pages along with all the other couples who planned to marry that summer, or who had just been married.

"We ought to go on," I whispered to Thierry, who was lying on his stomach, his chin resting on the ground, his eyes staring into space, all his senses concentrated in his round, very black ear. "It can't be here." I added, "Where can it hide?"

Younger frogs become disoriented or lost; they expose

themselves to dangerous conditions because they're so naive. The ability to protect oneself, to hide oneself, is learned behavior in almost all amphibians. The few *grenouilles du sang* left in the world, if there were any left, of necessity had to be adults. And it made no sense for an adult specimen to behave so imprudently.

"Please God, sir . . . "

I couldn't tell if he was praying, imploring his "mysteries," his *loas*, his impenetrable, nocturnal gods to put the frog in his path. I decided to wait another half hour, and not a second longer. All we had was tonight and tomorrow night, too few hours to take our leave of Casetaches Hill, and once we left, there was no other place to look. We were saying good-bye to Haiti too, and to the *Eleutherodactylus sanguineus.* Most difficult of all would be my call to Vaughan Patterson. Herpetologists don't understand certain things. You couldn't talk to Patterson about any subject except amphibians, he had nothing but contempt for colleagues who, when they were with him, alluded to anything as pedestrian, as trivial, as banal as a vacant chair at the university, a child's birthday, a parent's sickness. If I didn't capture the frog, what would I say when I called him at his laboratory in Adelaide, how would I explain that Haiti wasn't simply a place, a name, a mountain with a frog that had survived? How would I tell him about Cito Francisque, the man who had driven me off the Mont des Enfants Perdus? What would I say about the way they threw live animals onto their bonfires, about the dust and the stink, that unbearable, unspeakable, unfathomable stench? How would I describe the streets, the open sewers, the human shit in the middle of the sidewalk, the corpses at dawn, the woman whose hands were missing, the man whose face was missing? How would I make Patterson—dying of leukemia, his life hanging by the thread of scientific curiosity, rigor, and passion that connected him to this frog—how would I make him understand that Luc, the botanists' guide, had been buried without his feet and that Paul, Thierry's brother, was probably rotting somewhere, missing a piece of his body? God Almighty, how would I make him see that Haiti was disappearing, that the great hill of bones growing before our very eyes, a mountain higher than the peak of Tête Boeuf, was all that would remain?

"It's the devil," Thierry said in a stifled voice, "get down and see . . . "

He turned on his flashlight and I kept mine off. I followed the path of light he laid out for me, crawling without a sound, pushing myself along on my elbows, barely breathing, not lowering my head.

"Do you see it?"

The light stopped moving. There was a rock next to a small tree, a little grass at the foot of the trunk. I stood up to look, and froze.

"Tell me if it's a dream," Thierry stammered, "because I'm looking right at it."

The frog's back was to us, I saw its blazing dorsum and could clearly make out its paws, the toes lighter than the rest of the body. Motionless, it looked like a kind of poisonous flower, a fruit, a small, shining piece of viscera.

"What now, sir?"

I told him to keep on, he couldn't move the light now, the frog might jump away and disappear, we had to watch it until our eyes were burning, follow it wherever it went, die if we had to, as long as we didn't lose it. The *grenouille du sang* shifted one of its hind legs, but didn't move.

"It must be sick," Thierry whispered.

Then we were almost on top of it, we saw it give a short hop that didn't even carry it out of our field of vision. Only now it sat sideways, the light hit it obliquely and illuminated the silvery half-moon of its eye. As if I hadn't been moved enough by its presence, its abundant color, its stillness, now I could see the line, the tiny mirrorlike brilliance around the window to its inner life: an eye that shone with the blazing certainty of an omen.

"It's yours," Thierry encouraged me.

I told him I'd go around the bushes so I'd be at a better angle. He ought to stay where he was, focusing on it, all five senses concentrated on the animal.

"Don't worry."

I estimated that each step toward the frog would last a minimum of five or six seconds, and getting to the spot where I could reach it would take me three minutes at most. In fact, it took me a little longer, and in that time we heard it sing. Two short, powerful calls, its voice coming from deep inside, a clamor though no one was there, a despairing, isolated bubble that rose from the depths of its being.

"I've got it!"

It was an adult male, fairly old judging by the skin on his paws and head, disoriented by age. I felt as if I were holding an ancient survivor, a creature that had forgotten to die, or had taken refuge in a place so remote he hadn't heard the warning, if there was a warning, or the annhilation order, if that's what it was. I put him into the plastic bag filled with moss and ferns, then I placed the bag in the protected compartment I had prepared in my knapsack.

"Don't you think another one must be around here someplace?"

Thierry, who was shining his flashlight on me, smiled as if he were witnessing an event arranged ahead of time, the end of some damn joke.

"You know the answer. That's an old animal. There's no other frog, that's the last one."

Even so, we stayed on for a while. Thierry told me he would have to celebrate and pay his tribute to Papa Lokó, the lord of the trees, the bromeliads, all the grass living or dead: "The lord, sir, is the one who pisses the most on the mountain." He had a bottle of rum in his knapsack, he uncorked it and poured a stream on the ground, passed it to me so I could take a drink, and then he drank. We started back to camp. It was midnight and I thought Sarah would be asleep. We certainly were going to wake her, call her so she could see the *grenouille du sang* and have a generous drink from the bottle.

Sarah was awake, very pale, waiting for us. She hadn't slept at all because of the shooting, distant bursts of fire at first, something going on in Marfranc, then sounding closer; she wondered if they were already on their way up the mountain. Under these circumstances, she didn't show very much interest in our having trapped the *Eleutherodactylus sanguineus*.

"I have to stay," she said. I supposed she was imagining herself alone on the mountain. "Who will I bother up here?"

Thierry volunteered to go down. He knew some short-cuts that would get him into Marfranc before dawn. He would know how to move through the village, find out what was going on and what the situation was on the highway between Marfranc and Jérémie.

"I'll stay and work on the frog," I said; Thierry knew I had to preserve it.

"Tell it good-bye for me. That devil is sacred."

Sarah offered to help me. She claimed she wasn't sleepy, the shooting had made her wide awake, and she'd stay awake until Thierry came back. I think in her heart she was afraid something had happened to the Frenchman, though she didn't say so, she was incapable of displaying an emotion, she reminded me a little of Vaughan Patterson: She couldn't tolerate, or didn't care about, anything people said unless it had to do with cactus. While I was working on the frog, I mentioned that I would have to deliver it personally to Australia, the animal was going to a laboratory at the University of Adelaide.

"Well, when I find the *Pereskia*," she confessed, "and after I drop it off at the Botanical Garden, I'm going to go home, put on a movie, and eat breakfast while I watch the movie."

I started to laugh. I had been to the New York Botanical Garden only once, but I cared more about amphibians than anything else. And in that I was like Papa Crapaud: Frogs were my whole world, and the guts of a frog, as Thierry said, cannot enlighten a man. I resolved that when I went home, before I left for Adelaide, I'd settle my situation with Martha once and for all.

"I'm going to have breakfast after I deliver that cactus, even if it's eleven at night. I'm going to buy coffee and some toast and sit down in front of the TV set."

Then she told me she'd seen *Breakfast at Tiffany's* at least sixty times. Audrey Hepburn would drink her coffee and look in the show windows of a jewelry store; that soothed her. And what soothed Sarah was to watch Audrey Hepburn being soothed by jewels. It was like a chain. Or a dream inside a mirror.

Thierry returned in the morning. I recognized the hypnotized expression, the dumbfounded face, the comic stupor in his eyes: half of it a joke, the other half terror. I had learned this was a totally Haitian trait.

"Forget about Marfranc."

Sarah looked at me and I asked Thierry to sit down. He was still standing, like a casual visitor, like a phantom.

"We'll have to take some shortcuts from here to Jérémie. And go by boat from Jérémie to Port-au-Prince."

I asked about the car, the Renault that had left for the capital with Edouard, and the man from Marfranc behind the wheel, and Luc's corpse.

"They haven't come back," he said.

We began to pack. Thierry declared that the sooner we left, the better our chances of getting to Port-au-Prince safely.

"I'm staying," said Sarah.

Thierry stopped and looked at her. She was wringing her hands.

"Any time now I'm going to find the *Pereskia*. I don't think a woman up here will bother them, how could I bother them?"

I translated for Thierry, who was thoughtful for a moment and then went back to work, packing up all the jars, papers, and knapsacks. Once he turned to stare at Sarah, who seemed to be in a trance as she watched us pack.

"If she stays here, she'll be dead tomorrow. Take her

down by force, I tied up the foreigner's woman when I brought her down."

I tried to make her see reason. While we talked, all my gear had been organized: three backpacks in a pile at the door of the tent, a briefcase full of notes and half a dozen tapes. The voice of the *grenouille du sang* was there, that solitary, territorial call to a stupefied world, that unending, horrified song.

"I'm staying," Sarah said, definitively cutting off conversation.

I walked over to Thierry and thought out loud for a moment. I confessed I didn't know what else to say, what terrors or atrocities I should use to convince her.

"She doesn't want to move," I concluded.

"No woman wants to," said Thierry. "They all get confused. I told you before, you have to take them down by force. I could tie this one up too."

"We can't, Thierry, she isn't crazy."

"Yes she is. But Cito Francisque doesn't give a damn about that. He'll cut off her head anyway."

I didn't try again. I hung a couple of knapsacks over my shoulder, went over to Sarah and took her hand, held on to it intentionally, it was a hand that had groped its way through the forest, dug into the earth, the kind of roughened, grasping hand that so resembled mine. She hated good-byes but tolerated this one with equanimity. Then she turned away, picked up her knapsack, and walked off in the opposite direction; I stood there watching her until she disappeared along the mountain trails.

Thierry and I got away, making a long detour around Marfranc. He went into the village to buy food and find out the best route to Jérémie. It was quiet in town, absolutely quiet, in fact: They were holding wakes for six dead men in their own houses, but at least we managed to pick up more canned sardines and some liquor, and settled on how we'd get to Jérémie: We would pay a man to take us on his motorcycle. In the port at Jérémie we'd board the *Neptune*, a ferry that went directly to Port-au-Prince; Thierry had it all planned. We couldn't risk the highway; at the very least, that would mean losing all our gear, the packs with our equipment—he lowered his voice—"and the *grenouille du sang*."

We reached Jérémie in the middle of the night. We went straight to Thierry's house, but Carmelite and Mireille weren't there.

"Who knows if Paul ever showed up," he said. "They took away both women."

I had my first shower in days. And my first hot meal: Thierry cooked some broth and we ate it at dawn. Then we left; it wasn't a good idea to stay too long in that house. The *Neptune* sailed in the afternoon, and to pass the time we went to visit an old friend of his father's, one of the men who had been in his crew. While they talked I lay down on my sleeping bag and slept until Thierry shook me awake.

"Let's go to Port-au-Prince."

I folded up the bag, accepted a farewell glass of rum, and thought about Sarah. We walked down to the port; the boat looked like a disaster to me, but luckily it was a fairly short crossing. That stretch of ocean, which Thierry recalled as so unusual, so rough, had suddenly become our only escape. We settled in with all our gear, very close to the prow, and two men with a small goat came to sit beside us. One was barefoot, the other wore woven sandals; Thierry wore his sandals too, they were covered with mud. The boat began to move and again I felt sleepy; I took the pack with the *grenouille du sang* and wrapped the straps securely around my arm. Thierry sat looking at me and began a sad monologue, it was like a confession, he talked about the man he had stabbed to death and about his entire family. I realized that he too was a dying species, a trapped animal, a man who was too solitary.

"Be careful of the frog," was the last thing I heard him say, "hold tight to that devil."

※◇※ TWENTY ※◇※
Neptune

I tried to forget about killing that man. He deserved his punishment, he deserved even worse: Understand, he took a piece of chalk in his toes, because that's the only way, and he went to the Ireme, a great master in the Society, and drew a line on his back. The back of an Ireme is sacred, and he destroyed him, killed him, turned him into a woman. It's the worst thing that can happen to an abakuá.

They knew he had done it for revenge, they'd had a quarrel at work, they were both stevedores. But they called on me to kill him, it's something that either happens to you one day or never happens, and it happened to me, the Foundation pointed to me, they gave me the order, and I went to find him.

In the morning I came to a street called rue Chantal, that's where the apple stand is, the only place in Port-au-Prince that sells apples from France. I stopped in front of the pile of fruit, saw him coming, didn't know him but greeted him like a brother, and in my greeting I took his

life. I went straight back to my house and embraced
Blanche and my little boy Charlemagne, you have to do
that after you kill a man. The Society found me work in
Saint Michel de L'Attalaye, and I moved there with my
family.

The boys grew up, my two sons. Charlemagne became
a sailor, like his godfather, Jean Leroy, he fished for tuna
far from Haiti, and when he was a man he died in the
water, in the same net they used to pull out the fish, he
got caught in the ropes with another kind of fish, they
said he was trying to return it to the sea and the fish carried him down to the bottom. Honorat was the name we
gave to the twin who came out of his mother's womb
alive, and his bones didn't grow old either because he was
killed in a fight over a woman. So you see that I had children, but one by one I lost them. And in the end I left
Blanche. I discovered she had taken a dislike to me, an
anger that not even she could understand, maybe because
she gave birth to her babies for nothing, or because she
realized, over the years, that Frou-Frou was not like a
mother to me. She never was.

I left her in Saint Michel de L'Attalaye and went to live
with my brother Jean Pierre, there behind the garbage
dump I showed you that day. I was living a quiet life when
I heard that a foreigner, a frog hunter like Papa Crapaud,
was going around Port-au-Prince asking who could take
him up the mountain. You were the frog hunter, and this
is where the road ends, the road we traveled together, here
on the *Neptune*, what kind of name is that for a boat?

A man repeats all his roads, he repeats them without
realizing it, his illusion is that they're new. I have no more
illusions, but I do have to walk my own steps, the few I

have left, and you have to walk yours, and the woman who stayed up there and will be dead tomorrow, she will walk again on the path that is hers. Even Cito Francisque, as powerful as he is, has to repeat it all, from mountain to mountain, from blood to blood.

When Frou-Frou died I went to Jérémie to kiss the earth where she rested. Carmelite and Mireille brought some flowers to the burial, withered flowers, the only ones they could find that day. We were praying to her good angel, just before they put her into the ground forever, when the flowers that Carmelite was holding, and also the ones that Mireille was holding, began to lose their petals, a wind came and stripped them. The petals fell into the grave and it was like somebody touching a finger to my forehead. I remembered Papa Crapaud's burial and the little cones of rose petals Ganesha gave us. The dead also repeat their roads. The invisible finger touched my brow again and I forgot about the smell of dung and the stink of piss that disgusted me so much in Ganesha. I only remembered her prayer, Ganesha was dead and her ghost came to whisper in my ear:

"You, darkness, enfolding the spirit of those who ignore your glory."

I raised my head and knew that at the hour of my death I too should say those words. I repeated them for many days, I repeated them until I knew them all, they became part of my flesh and I know I'll never forget them.

I will see everyone I've been waiting for, probably everyone who loved me, I will stretch out my arms to them and speak to them slowly so they'll understand:

"You, darkness . . . "

Then they will show me the light.

In the mid-1970s, a significant decline was noted in the population of *Eleutherodactylus sanguineus*, a small, bright-red land frog found only in the mountainous regions of Hispaniola.

Ten years later, the frog disappeared from the Dominican Republic. At the same time, it was reported that the species was on the verge of extinction in Haiti, where only a few isolated specimens had been spotted on the Mont des Enfants Perdus, a mountain near Port-au-Prince.

In November 1992, the American herpetologist, Victor S. Grigg, made a field trip to this mountain but failed to find a single specimen of the *grenouille du sang*, the common name in Haiti for the *Eleutherodactylus sanguineus*.

Several weeks later, on the basis of private information that placed the frog on Casetaches Hill, at the westernmost tip of the island, Grigg traveled to this location, carried out an extensive search, and captured an adult male, which, according to Grigg's own notes, was the last of its species on earth.

On February 16, 1993, on the way to Port-au-Prince from the port of Jérémie, the ship carrying Grigg sank off the coast of Grand Goave. Nearly two thousand people died in the tragedy. The bodies of the scientist and his Haitian assistant, Mr. Thierry Adrien, were never recovered.

The last, carefully preserved specimen of the *grenouille du sang* was lost with them at sea.